CALIFORNIA CONNECTION 2

CALIFORNIA CONNECTION 2

CHUNICHI

Urban Books, LLC
1199 Straight Path
West Babylon, NY 11704

ISBN- 13: 978-1-61523-774-6

Printed in the United States of America

This is a work of fiction. Any references or similarities to actual events, real people, living, or dead, or to real locales are intended to give the novel a sense of reality. Any similarity in other names, characters, places, and incidents is entirely coincidental.

Distributed by Kensington Publishing Corp.

Dedication

This book is dedicated to my second mother,

Ives Wynter
November 8, 1954–January 24, 2009

May your loving memory live on forever.

Chapter 1

"Mad New Year"

Sasha

Click-click. I put a single bullet in the head of my chrome .22-caliber handgun, put on the safety, and then placed it in my purse. I clutched my purse and folded my arms to fight off the frigid winter air as I rushed toward Club Encore in an attempt to beat the crowd.

To my surprise, once I reached the front I was met by a swarm of people. It was pure pandemonium as I made my way toward the entrance. Noticing the attention of the crowd focused on a car entering the parking lot, I paused just long enough to get a glimpse of what was so interesting.

"Look at this bitch," I said, rolling my eyes when I realized it was Jewel and Touch pulling into the club parking lot. I screwed up my face, showing full disgust. My blood was boiling as I watched them step out of their

Maybach and onto the red carpet like they were the fucking king and queen of England. From the telltale red bottom of her shoes, I knew Jewel had on none other than Christian Louboutin.

Touch wore a suit, and I'm sure it was top of the line as well. I had to admit, he looked sexy as hell in it.

Suddenly, a flashback of the night we fucked consumed me. It was like I could feel his hands gripping my ass as he forced himself deep inside me. *Damn.* For a moment I felt my panties becoming a little moist from the combination of seeing him and reminiscing.

"Excuse me."

My moment of admiration was broken by a ghetto chick who bumped into me, pushing along with the crowd in a desperate attempt to get into the packed club. Under normal circumstances, I would have let this bitch have it, but this night I had more pressing issues, so that bitch got a pass.

I burned with envy as Touch and his bitch headed toward the entrance. I should have been his trophy wife, the queen beside him on the throne. All around them stood crowds of people calling and reaching out to them like the fucking paparazzi, while others just stood in awe like peasants, wishing they could have one moment in their shoes. No matter which crowd they were classified in, the people still went unnoticed by "the royal couple," as security guards forced people out of their way to open a clear path for Jewel and Touch to enter the club. The shit was so sickening.

Realizing I was amongst this crowd of peasants and

paparazzi, I inched my way toward the front of the line, which wrapped around the building.

"Excuse me, sweetie." I poked out my small but perky 34B breasts and called out to one of the bouncers who guarded the front door of the club, giving him my most seductive look. This fat-ass, baldhead, clean–looking dude just glanced at me and then turned his head. *Muthafucka*! I couldn't believe this guy.

Still determined to get in, I dug into my purse, by-passing my gun, and pulled out a hundred-dollar bill. One thing I knew for sure is that money talks. This time I didn't even bother calling out to him. I just walked toward the entrance as though I were part of the royal court.

The same bouncer said to me, "This is VIP, ma'am. Are you on the list?"

"Yes, I am," I said, sliding the money into his hand. Moments later, I was walking through the door with no search and no hassle.

I stood in awe as I entered the club. I couldn't believe the sight before me. Although I hated to admit it, Jewel and Touch were really on some celebrity shit. They had definitely taken things to the next level in VA. *Well, at least Jewel will have a hell of a farewell party*, I thought as I walked through the tight crowd, knowing I planned to make this night her last.

I watched the time as I made my way toward the VIP area. It was 11:15. I had forty-five minutes to make it to the back, where Touch and Jewel were partying. I wanted to be sure I was there to bring Jewel's new year in with a bang—literally. The crowd was going crazy to Busta Rhymes' "Arab Money" when I reached the bar. I purchased a glass of Nuvo and took it to the head to ease my nerves. Then, as an added prop, I bought a bottle of Ace of Spades, to look as though I belonged in the VIP area.

I knew it would be even harder getting past the security guard at the VIP section. There, niggas passed a hundred dollars all night to get in, so I wasn't sure that was going to fly this go-'round. After fighting a crowd of groupies, I finally made it to the entrance of the VIP. The time was now thirty minutes to midnight, so I needed to get in fast.

"Excuse me, hon," I said to the security guard to get his attention.

"Malibu?" He called me by my dance name, causing me to take a closer look at him.

This must be my lucky day. This gotta be a sign that the new year is gonna be my year. I let out a sigh of relief, realizing this guy was a bouncer at a club I used to dance at. I always felt dancing got me nowhere, and nothing but a few fast dollars, but this was one time it was an actual benefit.

"Hey, boo. How you been?" I gently caressed his arm as I spoke. "I'm trying to get back there and celebrate with my girl, Jewel. I just flew in from Atlanta, and I want to surprise her. I just bought this bottle, so we can pop it and bring in the new year together." I put on my best game, all the while flaunting my breasts and putting on a few flirtatious gestures.

4

The security guard stepped back and unhooked the velvet rope, allowing me to go through.

I headed toward the back of the VIP area and found a quiet spot in the cut, where I could go unnoticed. There I spotted a sexy chocolate dude who screamed the signs of money. Everything, from his designer labels to his blinding diamonds, said, "I am that nigga."

I couldn't take my eyes off his blinding, iced-out watch. If for nothing else but the diamonds, I had to have that nigga. I could picture him naked with nothing but jewelry—chocolate and diamonds, two of my favorites. I also noticed he stood alone. Since I had a few minutes to spare, I used this as an opportunity to possibly get to know him better.

"Hey, sexy," I said. "You look like you need some company."

"Oh yeah?" He looked my body up and down like he had X-ray vision and could see right through my Betsey Johnson dress.

"Yeah," I said with my sassiest attitude, rolling my neck.

"I'm kind of busy right now, but we can exchange numbers and get up a little later." He pulled out his cell phone, and I did the same.

"What's your name?"

"Calico," he said, and then began to read off his number.

"Calico?" I took a deep swallow, hoping I'd heard him incorrectly.

He spelled his name out to me, "*C-a-l-i-c-o*," confirming I'd heard him correctly.

His response floored me. My heart raced, and my breathing picked up. I tried all I could to keep my composure and to keep my shaking hand steady as I entered my number in his phone. I used the name Malibu to protect my true identity.

"Okay, baby, I'll be hitting you up. Enjoy your night, and Happy New Year." I tried to play it cool. I excused myself and rushed out of the VIP and headed to the bathroom. There I gathered myself. *Oh my God.* My brain was racing and I could see my chest moving up and down as I inhaled and exhaled. I didn't have asthma, but I surely felt like I was about to have a damn asthma attack.

As soon as Calico said his name, although I'd never seen him face to face, I knew exactly who he was. He was the same Calico that Jewel used to fuck with, the same Calico that I stole one hundred thousand dollars from months earlier. The most frightening part was, I didn't know if he knew who I was, and if he knew I had stolen his money. I didn't know if Jewel had put the blame on me, or exactly what she'd told him about his missing money.

I looked at my watch, and it was now five minutes to twelve. Regardless of what happened, I was at the club on a mission, and I planned to complete it. So, I pulled myself together. I took a moment to look into the mirror, applied some much-needed lip-gloss, fixed my hair then headed back to the VIP area.

Just as I got through the rope, the countdown to midnight began. I spotted Jewel and prepared to give her that long-awaited gift as I rushed in her direction.

The countdown ended, and the crowd yelled, "Happy New Year!" Everyone went wild, as money dropped from the ceiling.

I watched as Touch stood on his throne, throwing champagne over a crowd of groupies. They looked like scavengers as they dove for the dollars that fell around them. Others just looked on in envy.

No one even noticed me as I took my time inching closer and closer toward Jewel. When I came within a couple feet of her, I tiptoed my way directly behind her. With fire in my eyes, I took a deep breath then delivered. *Bam!* One to the back of her head and she was down.

Simultaneously, I heard a deafening boom. Frightened, I turned around to see a fearless Calico standing with a smoking gun in his hand and the same fire I had in my eyes earlier. People scattered in every direction, screaming.

"He's got a gun!"

"Get down!"

"Where's Kita Boo and Tynika?"

Within moments, the crowded VIP area was clear, and all I could see was two lifeless bodies on the floor. One belonged to Touch, and not far from him lay Jewel. I knew who was responsible for Jewel's downfall, and the sight of her actually brought a proud smile across my face. Now, Touch was a different story. I didn't see him get shot, but I damn sure saw the smoking gun.

Luckily for Jewel, I'd decided to deliver a bottle to her head, instead of a bullet. Her man wasn't as lucky, though. Although I'd shared the same fire in my eyes as Calico, I didn't have the same balls. Gunshots in a packed club on New Year's Eve could only lead to jail. Too many eyewitnesses. Hell, I wasn't no career murderer, but I at least knew that shit.

Frantic, I rushed out of VIP, nearly knocking over the security guard on my way. I ran out the side door of the club to get to my car and get the fuck out of dodge. Moments later, I was in my car, peeling out of the parking lot, running over the curb and nearly tearing out the whole bottom of my car.

I sped down Virginia Beach Boulevard toward the interstate, passing six cop cars headed in the opposite direction. I knew exactly where they were going, and I was relieved to know I'd broken out in just enough time.

It wasn't until I reached my hotel room that I felt safe. I kicked off my heels and flopped across the bed. Thanks to Calico drawing so much attention to himself, I was confident that I'd gotten away with murder. He'd set things up perfectly. Any onlookers would be convinced that he was responsible for Jewel and Touch's deaths.

"Damn! What a fucking night," I said to myself as I got comfortable under the blanket and reflected on the multitude of events that had taken place in such a short period.

I couldn't believe I'd actually witnessed Touch getting shot, or even worse, that I'd run into Calico. I pulled out my phone and flipped to his number. Initially I'd planned to erase it. I wasn't sure to what use I could put the number of a crazed murderer, but something in me said not quite yet. One thing was for sure: I had no plans on getting up with him. I had no intention of calling him and no intention of answering any of his calls. This was a dude that possibly killed a man by gunfire in front of an entire club and didn't give a fuck. I could only imagine what he would do to me if he knew I stole his money. I knew I had to get out of Virginia and back to Atlanta ASAP, but not before I got some much-needed rest.

At first I had a little trouble falling asleep, not because I'd hit Jewel in the head with the bottle, but because I wasn't quite sure if Calico would figure out who I was and come after me next. After an hour of tossing and turning, I finally dozed off to sleep.

The next morning, I was awakened by the sound of a ringing phone.

"Hello," I answered in a cracked morning voice.

"Sasha Williams?"

"Yes."

"This is the front desk. It's now twelve o'clock and past checkout. Will you be staying another day?"

"No. I'm leaving now." I hung up before the lady on the other end could respond.

I grabbed the remote from the nightstand and turned on the television. My heart dropped to my feet, and I gasped for air at the sight before me. I shook my head and rubbed my eyes then turned up the volume to make sure what I was witnessing was real. And real it was. I panicked when I saw my face on the television screen.

"Police are investigating the shooting and felonious assault of a popular Virginia Beach couple. They are asking for your help in locating the whereabouts of Sasha Williams, the primary suspect in the crime."

I rushed to gather my things so I could get out of the hotel and on the road to Atlanta.

Before I could finish packing, I heard a forceful knock on the door, followed by a gruff bellow. "Virginia Beach police!"

I knew exactly what they wanted. Knowing how they moved and fearing for my life, I didn't even try anything crazy. One false move and they would swear I was reaching for a weapon, and my ass would be dead, twenty to thirty shots to the torso.

"I'm opening the door," I yelled as I unlocked the door. "I'm not resisting."

Several police officers rushed in, busting through the door with guns drawn. They threw me on the floor and slapped the cuffs on me in a single motion that seemed to take only one second.

"Sasha Williams, you have the right to remain silent. Anything you say can and will be used against you in a court of law. You have the right to an attorney . . ." The officer read me my Miranda rights.

"Yeah, yeah, yeah. Fuck you and Miranda! And that can go on record," I snapped as they lifted me from the floor and directed me out the door.

The ride to the Virginia Beach jail was long and uncomfortable. I sat slumped sideways, with my hands still cuffed, in the crammed backseat of the police car. I actually was relieved when we reached the station. I was ready to just get this whole ordeal over with.

From the car, I was escorted straight to the interrogation room and left freezing like a piece of meat in a freezer. I sat alone for forty-five minutes, shivering in this small room with nothing but a table and three chairs. I never quite understood the purpose of having the room below zero or the purpose of leaving you in the room alone for so long.

Finally, a man walked in who introduced himself as Detective Tarver. Almost to the point of going stir crazy, I welcomed the tall, husky, bald-headed white man, who seemed like he should have been playing some sort of contact sport instead of being a detective.

"Sasha Williams, you're being charged with two counts of attempted murder," the detective said as my mind wandered elsewhere.

What the fuck? Attempted murder? You mean to tell me that bitch ain't dead? My first reaction was one of disappointment, but then I really thought about what was being said to me. *Two counts of attempted murder, Sasha. You going to jail, bitch, and you ain't never getting out.* My heart palpitated, and I felt dizzy as I registered exactly what this man was telling me. Okay, with respect to Jewel, of course, I knew I was guilty, and there was no way around it. But, Touch, oh, hell no. That wasn't my charge, and I wasn't wearing that shit for nobody.

"Do you understand your rights and the counts you are being charged with?" the detective asked.

I'd missed all the information he'd said in between, and although I was still in shock, I just answered, "Yes, sir."

"Now, I know you're not a bad person, Sasha. You're a mother of two, and I know you would hate to lose your kids behind this. So I'm here to help you."

I knew the detective was lying. He didn't give a fuck about me or my kids. I'd seen this same scenario one too many times on the A&E series, *The First 48*. I knew what was coming next. He wanted me to help him, and he would help me.

I played along. "Please don't take me away from my kids," I pleaded.

"Well, here's the thing. We know we have enough information to charge you. That's no question. We have a security guard that identified you. He said you all had a conversation minutes before the incident, and you nearly knocked him over when you were fleeing the scene."

"Oh yeah?" I said, knowing exactly who he was speaking about. I couldn't believe that bitch-ass nigga from the strip club had turned me in. I guess he needed a good look in hopes of going from a nothing as a bouncer to a bitch-ass police officer.

"Yep, and right now, both of the victims are in critical condition. If they die, you could be looking at murder, and you will never see your kids again. I don't want that to happen to you, so I'm willing to help you, if you're willing to help me."

The detective gave almost the same spiel I'd hear on *The First 48* time and time again. It was almost comical. I had to wonder if that was a speech all cops learned in the academy.

"So what do I have to do?" I asked, continuing to play along.

Detective Tarver laid out the deal. "There's a major drug ring in Virginia Beach that revolves around Jewel, Touch, and Calico, and we know you were longtime friends with Jewel. So, what information can you give us to bring down their operation? Your cooperation in helping us bring them down can determine the outcome of your charges."

Seeing this as the perfect opportunity to kill two birds with one stone—getting rid of Jewel and Calico—I readily agreed. I hated Jewel and wanted her out of the picture, and I didn't know just how safe I was with Calico, seeing that I'd stolen his one hundred grand.

"Okay. I'll tell you what I know," I told him. "Calico was the main supplier. He brought cocaine from California and flooded the entire seven cities. Touch was his right-hand man, and together they were killing the drug game. But when Jewel got hooked up with the True Mafia Family, better known as TMF, Touch ended up using them as a new link, cutting Calico out.

"Jewel met the head guys in TMF through ghostwriting. They were coming out with a first-time album, and they hired her to ghostwrite a few songs on it. She used the power of brains and beauty to get in good with them. Then when she got her advance money, she purchased some weight from them and gave it to Touch to get rid of. She had it all planned out from the beginning.

"From that point on, money been constantly flowing. But Touch's big come-up brought beef between him and Calico. He ultimately stabbed Calico in the back and stole all his customers."

The detective continued to fish for information. "Do you have any phone numbers, addresses, or can you give us any other people that may be involved in this ring?"

Careful to tell the detective just enough to ease his hunger, but not enough to incriminate myself, we had a deal. By the end of our interrogation session, I had told Detective Tarver that Calico was Touch's shooter and submitted a written statement describing the events from that night.

When it was all said and done, I'd given Detective Tarver what he wanted, and we had a deal. I ended up being charged with only felony assault, but in turn, I would have to testify against Calico as an eyewitness to the shooting. I can't lie, that shit made me nervous as hell, but a bitch had to do what she had to do to save her ass.

Initially, my thoughts had been that Jewel was lucky I hadn't shot her ass, but in the end, it was lucky for me. Although everything in me wanted to see her in a casket, I knew shooting her in the club would have been too risky. Calico, on the other hand, wasn't as smart.

Chapter 2

"Home Sweet Home"

Calico

It never felt so good to be back in Cali. A nigga was dead broke, and every dime I owned was on the streets, waiting to be collected. I was really starting to feel the effects of Touch's little business taking the rise. I had plenty of product I'd bought from across the border, but no one to push that shit. The Mexicans were loading up cats on the West Coast with cocaine, so they could get my same shit for equal or better, making it impossible to move any weight on my side. It was those niggas on the East Coast that would pay top dollar, but that snake-ass Touch had swiped each and every one of my customers. It was hard to even get rid of my shit on the East Coast at this point.

I thought back to when everything was gravy. I would get the shit from the Mexicans and then hook up with my niggas on the East Coast. In only a matter of days I could get rid of everything. Back then, Touch would take half of the work off my hands off the buck. But then that nigga fucked up the business, had to go and get all pussy-whipped and shit. That put me in a hell of a predicament with the Mexican Mafia. I knew those niggas didn't play when it came to their money, so I used every dime to pay them back. A true soldier always knows it's money before bitches.

I was slowly building my money back up though. I can't lie, shit was real, and I ain't even have a hundred dollars to my name, but a nigga felt good to know he was about to be back on top. Putting Touch to rest was one definite way to assure my rise. After I put those hot balls in his ass, I broke out of Virginia the next morning. I hit up one of my little soldiers back in VA to give me the word on the streets.

"Yo!" Poppo answered.

I got right to business. "What's the word on that side?"

"You gotta work on your aim, duke."

"Fuck you mean, bitch nigga?" I asked, slightly insulted by Poppo's statement.

"Bitch?"

I could tell, by his tone, Poppa didn't take much liking to the name-calling, but I wasn't letting up. "You heard me, nigga. And watch your fucking tone." I was the fucking boss, so I needed to make sure he recognized that when speaking to me.

"Whatever you say, duke. But, anyway, that nigga still breathing," Poppo said still with a slight attitude, but he didn't have the balls to act on his aggravation.

"Hell nah!" I couldn't believe the shit I was hearing. I never missed a target.

"Yeah, dawg, that shit was on the news. They say that nigga in critical condition. And I hear they got that bitch Sasha locked up."

"Sasha? Who the fuck is Sasha?" I asked Poppo, the name sounding familiar to me.

"She that bitch that used to roll tight with Jewel. But the crazy shit is, she popped Jewel in the head with a champagne bottle that same night at the club. I hear Jewel in a fucking coma. That bitch, Sasha, picture was on the news and everything, dawg."

"I can't believe the shit I am hearing right now. You mean to tell me that bitch stood right beside me and I ain't even know that was her? Man, I'm fucking slipping. The bitch came over and tried to holla at a nigga; we exchanged numbers and everything. I got the number in my phone right now. No wonder the bitch started to look all sick and pale in the face, like she'd seen a fucking ghost when I told her my fucking name. She real lucky. That bitch has no idea how close she was to catching one of those hot balls along with Touch. One thing fo' sho', next time, that bitch won't slip away from me." Burning up inside with anger, I ended the call with Poppo and rolled a blunt.

After smoking on some high-grade, I dozed off to sleep.

I was wakened by the constant ringing of my cell phone. I looked at the caller ID. It was my attorney, Natalia Bergetti. Worry hovered over me as I answered the phone. She and I had a hate-love relationship. I hated being brought on charges and loved it when she got my ass off.

She called me by my government name. "Michael?"

"What's up? I know it gotta be bad news for you to be calling me."

"Hate to say it, but yes, it's pretty bad. I just got word from one of my contacts that you're being charged with attempted murder on Trayvon Davis, AKA Touch. And to make matters worse, they have an eyewitness. She was the original suspect, but I'm sure she worked out a deal with the detectives to lessen her charges, if she agrees to testify against you. You know they have been out for you for some time now, so if they can't get you on drug charges, they will certainly go for murder. They just want to see you put away a very, very long time."

"A'ight." I let out a deep sigh and then added, "Well, I'll be there to check you in a few days. Let me sort some things out first." I ended the call.

After I hung up the phone, I wondered if my reign as the Teflon man had run out. One thing I did know for sure though. A nigga wasn't turning hisself in. Those bitch-ass Virginia Beach cops was gonna have to find me.

I had a fucking instant headache as I processed everything that was going on. I was already awaiting trial on a fucking Racketeer Influenced and Corrupt Organizations Act charge, better known as a RICO charge, and now attempted murder. I was pretty confident my attorney could work out the RICO charge with a plea or something, but a witness to that attempted murder was no joke.

That shit was real! I'm sorry, but a nigga just wasn't built for a long bid in the penitentiary. Having a guard with horrible breath telling me what to do, being given slop for meals that even an animal wouldn't eat, beating my dick to a *XXL* magazine and having my momma and kids coming up for visits with tears in their eyes wasn't an option for me. I would pay any price for freedom, and believe me, my attorney wasn't cheap.

Besides, I already knew who their little eyewitness was. It had to be that bitch Sasha. Without an eyewitness, they had no case. So, with that said, I knew what I had to do. It was official. That bitch Sasha had to be dealt with. I knew I would be making a trip to Virginia real soon, but first, I needed to go relieve some tension and get these two monkeys off my back.

I decided to go pay my baby mother a little visit. I hopped in my car and headed to her crib unannounced.

" 'S up?" I greeted Corrin, my baby mother, as I walked in on her just in time for dinner. She was cooking fried chicken.

"Use that house key I gave you for emergencies only," she barked at me putting emphasis on the word *emergencies*.

"Whatever." I smacked her on the ass. "Where my kids at?"

"At swimming lessons with my mother, like every Tuesday. If you were an active father, you would know that. And I repeat, that key is for *emergencies* only."

I wasn't trying to hear shit Corrin was saying. I had to give it to her though, she was a true ride-or-die chick. She would rob, stab, or shoot a nigga for me. What she truly wanted was to tie me down, but never that. I wasn't that kind of nigga.

"Don't I pay for your rent in this bitch every fucking month?" I snapped back at her.

"Yeah," she replied, facing me, rolling her eyes.

"If something is broke around here, don't I fix it 'cause your sorry-ass landlord don't give a fuck?"

"Yeah."

"A'ight. Then give me the respect that I deserve, woman," I said, coming closer in the kitchen.

"Nigga, spend more time with your son and daughter. After you tote them around the mall, get them something to eat and some toys, you ready to bring them home. It's more to being a daddy than material shit. You care more about popping fucking bottles in the club than being a father. So be a real daddy and start paying my lights, cable, phone and car payment, then I will start showing you more respect around here. And come in here again unannounced like that and I will change the locks."

That shit she was saying was going in one ear and out the other. Every day was the same shit, but this day I wasn't in the mood. All I wanted was some weed, pussy, and food, and that's what I planned on getting.

"Corrin, I don't need this shit from you today. I already got a headache. Your mouth is going to make it turn into a fucking migraine!" I yelled, confronting her.

I turned her around, pulled down her shorts, popped off her G-string, and bent her over. She smelled like sweet vanilla. I quickly loosened my belt and pulled down my jeans and boxers.

"Hmm, I knew you wanted you some pussy. Hurry up before my mom comes with the kids."

I smacked her ass, spread her cheeks, and pushed my dick into her wet pussy. That was one of the greatest benefits of having a baby moms—guaranteed pussy anytime I wanted. Yeah, Corrin bitched and complained about every little thing, but she was always willing to open those legs for me, day or night.

Chapter 3

"Soldier Status"

Poppo

After talking to Calico I was fucking vexed. I had stood by that nigga's side for years, never deceiving him, stealing from him, or trying to shave off his profit. There was no other nigga that had his back like me, and this was the thanks I get? Not wanting to sit and dwell on him and his bullshit, I decided to go to the barbershop and kick it with some of my niggas and fuck with some of the freak bitches that hang up there.

"Damn, nigga! Fuck wrong with you? Coming in the shop like you wanna kill niggas and shit," Mike, one of the barbers, said as soon as I walked in the place.

My feelings must have been written all over my face. "Ain't shit, man. Who in the chair next?" I asked, still a little aggravated.

"You." Mike brushed the hair from the chair, using a cape, then threw it around me.

Once in the chair, and out of earshot of the public, I began to fill Mike in.

"Nah, duke, it ain't no beef shit. I just got off the phone with that nigga Calico, and that nigga be talking to me like I'm some little bitch. He needs to start respecting men. You feel me?"

"Right, right." Mike didn't say much. Him, like most niggas, was too afraid to curse Calico.

The more I thought about things it really started to get under my skin. I had to wonder what the fuck this nigga took me for. After everything I'd done for homie, all the fucking wars we'd been through and I had this nigga back, this nigga was still talking to me like I was some little nothing-ass nigga. I'd been past the toy soldier status. A nigga had his wings now, but Calico couldn't see it. But whether he chose to see it or not, I knew I wasn't gonna be his "gofer" for too much longer. It was definitely time for change.

Although I'd never crossed Calico before, I was really considering it. I was making just enough money to get by working with him. It was time for me to make a come-up. I figured the next time that nigga gave me some shit to deliver, or some money to collect, I was gonna take that shit and flip and make a little money off of it, then pay him. As long as I did that shit quickly, he would never know the difference. After a few flips, I would have enough money on my own to start buying some weight.

Chapter 4

"Living Nightmare"

Jewel

My eyes opened suddenly as I was jolted out of my sleep from the nightmare that kept playing over and over in my head. I waited for my eyes to focus. Slightly disoriented, I could hear a constant beeping and faint voices in the background as well. I looked around, slowly focusing my eyes, and realized I was in a hospital.

That's when the realization hit me that I hadn't been dreaming at all. There really was an accident. I felt like I was beginning to live out my nightmare. I started to panic. *Had I been shot? Where is Touch?* I touched my head and screamed out in pain. *Oh my God! I was shot in the head! Am I retarded? Can I walk? I need a mirror! Oh my God! Please, where's the mirror?* I felt like I was going crazy. I looked around the room frantically for a mirror. I couldn't move due to all the different tubes that were attached to me, so I called for help.

"Help me! Please help me!" I began to yell out for a nurse.

Seconds later a nurse rushed in. "Hi, Miss Diaz. Glad to see you up and alert. I'm Misty, and I'll be your nurse today. Is everything okay?" she asked calmly.

"No. What happen to my head? Was I shot? I need to see a mirror," I said, still in a panic. Months earlier I'd taken a nasty blow to the head, and it was not nice. I was all swollen and black and blue for days. I refused to go through that again.

"Just calm down, Miss Diaz. You were not shot. You were hit in the head with a bottle. You have been in a coma for two days," Nurse Misty explained.

I asked the next most important question. "What about my boyfriend, Trayvon Davis? Where is he?"

"Your boyfriend isn't doing as well as you are. He's in our intensive care unit."

"Oh God! This can't be happening," I said, realizing again my nightmare was reality. "He was shot, wasn't he?"

"Yes, he was. He was shot in the stomach, and the bullet exited through his back, damaging quite a few vital organs in the process. He's currently in critical condition."

As I listened to the nurse and registered what she was saying, my chest began to tighten, and I felt like I couldn't breathe. "I think I'm gonna pass out," I said to her between pants, and the slow, constant, beeping sounds in the background picked up in pace.

Misty tried to coach me back to a normal breathing

pattern. "You're panicking. Just relax and take some deep breaths."

"I have to see him, please," I begged the nurse.

"I'll see what we can do. Just give me a few minutes to talk with the doctor." Misty then exited the room.

I watched as she walked out. Misty was a young nurse, a nice-looking black girl, dressed in Baby Phat scrubs, with a big phat ass to match. I'm usually good at judging character, and she looked liked one of those get-money chicks. With that in mind, I needed to keep her far from my man.

"Ouch!" A streaking pain ran through my head, diverting my attention back to my injury.

I couldn't believe what was going on. I couldn't understand how we went from a night of celebrating the New Year, to Touch being shot and me in a coma. The more I played that night over and over in my head, the more the pieces of the puzzle began to come together. Before long I'd recapped the entire night in my head, and I knew exactly what had gone down. I was sure Calico had shot Touch, and Sasha had hit me in the head. Now that I knew the deal, I knew exactly what I had to do. Calico and Sasha had to pay.

Misty returned to the room with a wheelchair. "Miss Diaz?"

"Yes?"

"I'm gonna take you to see Mr. Davis. The doctor wanted you to wait until he was able to come in and do a quick examination, but I convinced him to let me go ahead and take you to see your boo."

We both laughed at her usage of the word *boo*.

"Thanks, girl," I said to Misty as though we were long-time friends. "I really appreciate it."

"Oh, trust me, I understand. I was in your place once. Me and my man were in a car accident, and when I came to, all I wanted to do was see him. So I feel your pain." Misty parked the chair next to my bed and began to prepare me for my trip.

My opinion suddenly changed about her. Instead of looking at her as another greedy street-bitch, I actually saw her as a pretty cool female. She helped me out of bed, and minutes later, I was comfortable in the wheelchair.

Misty swept me off to Touch's room. As we entered the room, I instantly felt the same tightness I'd felt in my chest earlier, and again, I began to struggle to breathe. The sight of a lifeless Touch with tubes coming from every direction and constant beeps of the monitor and inflation of the breathing machine was just too overwhelming for me.

"Why are there so many tubes? What's going on?" I asked Misty between my tears and pants.

Misty rolled me right next to Touch's bed, and I grabbed his hand as she explained his current state and what the different tubes were for. My heart literally ached as I watched the love of my life lay before me unconscious.

"Just leave me here," I said to Misty. "I want to spend some time with him alone."

"No problem, but I must tell you. Detectives have been up here several times to speak with you and Mr. Davis.

They asked that we give them a call when you all regain consciousness."

"I'm really not interested in speaking to no DT right now, or ever for that matter." I kissed my teeth and rolled my eyes simultaneously.

"Well, I'm not going to call them, but I just wanted to make you aware." Misty smiled.

"Thank you so much. You are so understanding. I owe you." I smiled back and then diverted my attention to Touch.

"I love you so much, baby." I caressed his hand as I spoke to him. "I know you can make it out of this. Come on, Touch. I need you here. Your twin girls need you here. Too many people are depending on you, baby." I knew Touch loved his daughters with all his heart, and if anyone could inspire him to fight, it would definitely be them.

I laid my head beside him on the bed. I could still smell the fresh scent of his Vera Wang cologne. "I love you, Touch," I constantly whispered to him until I dozed off to sleep.

The next day I was discharged from the hospital with enough pain pills to sedate a horse. I had fifteen staples straight down the center of the back of my head. When I got home, all I could think about was Touch. After calling his mother, situating things at home, and taking a much-needed shower, I got in my car and headed back to the hospital, no more than two hours after I'd left. That's where I spent each day—by Touch's side— until he regained consciousness.

Chapter 5

"Sad Reality"

Touch

"Aaaahhh fuck!" My body ached with so much pain, and it throbbed as though I'd been hit by a fucking bus. I slowly opened my eyes and struggled to figure out where I was.

I heard a familiar voice say, "Touch, baby," and felt a gentle touch on the side of my face.

I turned to my left side to see Jewel sitting next to me. "What?" I struggled to talk but noticed something was preventing me.

"No, no, baby, don't try to talk," Jewel said to me. "There's a tube in your mouth." She then called for the nurse.

I noticed I felt extremely thirsty, as I took the time to examine my body and things started to register. It seemed like I had tubes coming from every hole in my body. I had tubes coming from my mouth, arm, and even my dick.

Shit was really starting to sink in. I remembered getting shot at the club. Although I was shot in a matter of seconds, the events seemed to have occurred in slow motion. I remembered seeing Calico dip in his waist and me thinking, *This nigga got a fucking gun*, knowing he was going to shoot me. My first instinct was to push Jewel to the floor to get her out of danger. The last thing I remembered was locking eyes with her, and then feeling extreme pain to my stomach. And from the way things were looking from that hospital bed, Calico had really fucked me up. But the one mistake that bitch nigga made was to leave me breathing.

Minutes later, the nurse walked in. After checking my vitals and a quick exam, she removed my breathing tube from my mouth. My first request was water. After quenching the severest case of cotton mouth a nigga could ever experience, I began to ask the thousand questions that had been plaguing my mind.

"How many times was I shot?" I forced out the first question.

"Once," Jewel answered right away.

"Where?"

"In the stomach and exiting out your back," Jewel said, confirming exactly what I'd suspected.

"So, how bad is it?"

I watched Jewel's expression change after I asked that question. That was a sure sign a nigga was fucked up.

Jewel came with some bullshit answer. "Baby, don't worry about all that. You're alive, that's all that matters."

"Yo, this me you talking to, Jewel. Don't give a nigga the runaround. What's the deal? Am I paralyzed or something?"

"No, you're not, but you're gonna have to go through extensive rehab to learn to walk again." Jewel dropped her head and began to cry.

There was nothing I could say. So many emotions were hitting me at one time. I was so fucking vex that I let this nigga Calico take so much from me. I was hurt that Jewel had to see me go through this. I felt like shit because, at the time, a nigga was like a fucking baby. Somebody had to feed me, bathe me, change me, and I even had to learn to walk again. What good was I? I didn't know if you could even consider somebody in that state as a man.

"I'm gonna kill Calico," I said, pure hate in my heart and eyes.

Jewel tried her best to divert my anger to positive energy. "Baby, please don't talk like that. Don't even focus on him. Put your energy into your health. We just need to get you better."

"Matter of fact, why are you even here? I can't do shit for you. If I can't walk or even feed myself, I definitely can't fuck you. Plus, we both know how you love money. If I can't grind, the money will be gone soon, which means you'll be out looking for the next cat. Ain't no point in waiting. Just leave now. You ain't gotta stick around because you feel sorry for me, or because you feel like it's the right thing to do. Haul ass!"

"Touch, why are you acting like that? I've been here

by your side every day and night for an entire week while you lay here unconscious. I love you and I'm not giving up on you, no matter what!" Jewel cried.

"Did you not hear me? Get the fuck out, Jewel!" I then began to yell for the nurse. "Nurse!"

The nurse rushed in. "Yes, Mr. Davis?"

"Could you have her leave?"

"Mr. Davis, she's been here by your side every day and night."

"So what? Are you gonna make her leave, or do I need to call security?"

Misty hesitated before speaking. "I'm sorry, Jewel. I have to respect his wishes," she said reluctantly. "I'm afraid I'm gonna have to ask you to leave."

"Misty, I'm not going anywhere. He's just upset right now. This is a lot for him to handle."

"Jewel, if he calls security, you won't ever be able to re-enter the facility."

With tears in her eyes and hurt written all over her face, Jewel gathered her things and headed toward the door. "I love you, Touch, and I refuse to give up on you, even if you give up on yourself. I'm standing by your side, no matter what." Her words were followed by the sound of the door closing behind her.

The next few weeks were filled with intense rehabilitation and constant questioning by detectives. At times, I didn't know if the DTs were trying to find my shooter or get up in my business. On the real, this one detective was making me feel like I was the fucking criminal instead of the victim. They kept asking if I knew my shooter.

Of course, I lied and said no. Shit like this had to be handled on the streets. There was no getting the cops involved. But they just weren't happy when I told them I didn't know my shooter. From there they tried to insinuate it was drug activity that provoked my shooter to come after me, like a drug deal gone bad or some shit. These niggas had to be crazy if they thought I would admit to something like that. Needless to say, after two or three of these bullshit interrogations, all contact was off when it came to the police.

Jewel and I had made up. She didn't give up on me. I swear, if she hadn't done just like she promised and stayed by my side the entire way, I would have fucking lost it. In fact, she showed me more love than I'd ever expected. She'd shown me so much that I knew I had to give her all of me. I had to give her a part of me that no other woman ever had. There were times when I felt like shit, less than a fucking man, and I took that frustration out on her, but no matter what, she still was there encouraging me. She was at my bedside each day, feeding me at mealtime. Although she had no proper training, she would beat the nurses to giving me a bath and assisting me to the bathroom. I always knew Jewel was that down-ass bitch, but now I felt like I owed her big time.

Chapter 6

"Here Comes the Bride"

Jewel

"**C**ome on, baby." I helped Touch out of bed and into a standing position so that he could use his walker.

He had made a lot of progress over the past few weeks. He'd gone from being totally dependent to walking, bathing, eating, dressing, and basically doing everything on his own. Although Touch was recovering, I still had a deep hatred for Calico, and I wasn't going to be happy until he paid for his deed.

Touch's mother walked through the front door.

"Hey, Ma!" I said.

Touch's mother would come over periodically to give me a break. That gave me an opportunity to do any errands I may have. I refused to leave Touch alone until I was sure he could bust a nigga ass if he had to. Until then he would never be alone. I'd purchased extra guns

and placed them throughout the house for added protection. I'd even gone as far as to teach his mom how to
shoot. This nigga Calico had just tried to take Touch's
life, and there was no way I was gonna take a chance of
him coming back to finish the job.

"Okay, baby, I'll be right back." I kissed Touch and
then headed toward the front door prepared to set the
alarm on my way out. Although we lived in a prominent
high-end neighborhood, crime had no address, so I
needed to protect my man at all costs.

"Wait!" Touch called out as though he was in pain.

"What's wrong, baby?" I said in a panic.

"Come sit next to me." Touch patted on a stool at the
breakfast bar next to him. "I wanted to wait 'til my mom
was here before I did this."

Confused, I slowly walked toward him and sat on the
stool as he requested. I watched as he struggled to dig
an item from out of his pocket. I immediately reached
out to assist him.

"No, baby," he said, resisting. "I got it." He then finally pulled out a small box. "This isn't the way I
dreamed of doing things, but this can't wait any longer.
You've shown me love that no other woman, other than
my mother, has ever shown me. We've shared good and
bad times, and between it all, you stood your ground as
my ride-or-die chick. Jewel, I love you, baby, and I can
never repay you for your loyalty, but I can give you all of
me for the rest of my life. If you would accept, I would
love for you to be my wife. Will you marry me?"

My eyes filled with water, and it felt like someone was

literally tugging at my heart. "Yes, baby. Of course, I will be your wife."

We kissed each other passionately.

My ring was beautiful. Touch had outdone himself. As soon as I'd seen the name Harry Winston, I knew there was no way I could be disappointed. He was a celebrity jeweler, so I knew Touch couldn't go wrong with him. I opened the box to see a 14-karat white gold princess and baguette matching ring and band set with a total weight of eight carats. I immediately placed the ring on my finger and admired it, leaving the band in the box for our actual wedding day.

"Well, it looks like I'm finally getting my wish," Touch's mom said. She'd always wanted me as a daughter-in-law.

Way back when Touch and I were truly platonic friends, I could remember his mother constantly saying, "Boy, I sure wish you were my daughter-in-law."

"Now get out of here and go do your wifely duties. Get me some groceries, woman!" Touch said in a playful tone.

I grabbed my Gucci bag and headed out the door and made my way to Wal-Mart. Like always, the Wal-Mart parking lot was full, and the store was busy like a damn nightclub. I breezed my way through the aisles of the store, picking up items and checking them off my grocery list.

"Yo, Jewel," someone called out to me.

I turned around to see one of Calico's boys that went by the name Poppo standing before me. I unzipped my purse that sat in the child seat of the shopping cart. I wanted easy access to my gun in case I needed to shoot this nigga.

"Yeah?" I responded with an attitude. I didn't know what type of shit he was on, and I didn't want to make the mistake of showing fear.

"What's good with you, baby girl? Still looking good, I see."

I could tell by his body language and his words that he wasn't on no beef shit. In the past, he had tried to get with me, but since Touch had gotten shot, I didn't know what to expect or who could be trusted.

"Whatever, nigga." I blew him off then continued to look for Touch's favorite cereal, Fruity Pebbles.

"Why you keep blowing me off? I been trying to holla at you for a minute now."

I was just about to diss the hell out of this nigga, but then it hit me. Poppo was obviously one of those niggas that was weak for pussy. He had been trying to get with me since I was dating Calico. Every time Calico would send him to pick up some shit from me or to deliver me some money or anything, he would always make a pass at me. One time he even grabbed my ass. I figured, if he would stab his boy in the back during that time, why not do it now? Literally, that is. Plus, I knew firsthand how Calico treated his boys. He treated them like shit. I knew I could easily get in Poppo's head, so I executed.

"Yeah, you have, Poppo, but I'm a boss bitch, and I

need a boss by my side. I can't have no nigga that's being bitched out every day by some other nigga that thinks he's the boss."

"Man, fuck that nigga! I'm trying to do a little something on my own, so I can break off from that nigga now. He be trying to play niggas for a little bitch, and I'm getting tired of that shit."

Poppo's simple ass played right into my little game when he said exactly what I wanted to hear.

"So you think all you need is a little drug connect to get away from Calico? Hell, if that's all it takes, I can put you on to a connect, but Calico will kill your ass if he knew you was trying to do your own thing. That shit makes you his competition."

"Man, I'll deal with Calico."

Poppo's words were music to my ears.

"Okay, look . . . this is the deal. You know Touch is fucked up, so he ain't even fucking with the drug game right now. So I'm gonna need a new boss by my side. If you can get rid of Calico to assure we won't have problems, I will put you on to my connect, and me and you can build a new empire of our own."

"Done deal. Say no more. How can I reach you?"

Poppo's weak ass had fallen right into my trap. Just like the average nigga, he was weak for pussy. I knew I could tell him anything and have him eating out of the palm of my hand. Sure, I made him feel like he was the man and I was gonna be by his side, but it was only to get what I wanted, which was Calico out of the way and my man safe. What better way to have Calico killed than to have his own boy do it?

Poppo and I exchanged phone numbers, and I finished up my grocery shopping excited as a kid on Christmas.

Chapter 7

"Indecent Proposal"

Poppo

"**D**amn right!" I said to no one in particular as I walked back to my car in the parking lot of the Wal-Mart shopping center.

Running into Jewel was a coincidence, but the offer she made had to be a sign that it was time to break away from Calico. But, still, I had to wonder if this bitch was for real. I must admit, her offer did seem too good to be true. Was this bitch trying to set me up? After all, my man did just try to kill her nigga. *Maybe, once I get Calico out the way, I would be her next man.* All kinds of shit was running through my head, but fuck it! I needed the come-up. It was whatever.

Once I got to the crib, I couldn't get that shit off my mind. This would be the perfect fucking come-up. I could be on top, and I knew that's all I needed to get Jewel. I'd wanted that ass for a long time and it looked like my time was finally coming. I stayed up late watching episodes of *The First 48* and eating pizza and drinking Heineken, which eventually got a nigga tired as hell. I slowly began to doze off to sleep.

"Poppo, I'm going to ask you this, one time," Jewel stated as she handed me a glass of Nuvo.

She was dressed in a red wife-beater and torn, tight-ass jeans that looked to have been painted on her. And, gotdamn, that ass was phat! We definitely weren't at my place or hers. Instead, it looked as if we were in one of those uppity expensive hotels like the Westin or Loews or something. The room was huge.

I lifted my head from the king-size bed to see pink roses scattered all over the carpet. A Jacuzzi was to the right of me. A tray of all kinds of cheeses, meats and fruits were to the left of me on a table. Yeah, I could get used to this kind of lifestyle. Jewel was definitely high-class and high-maintenance, but a nigga wasn't complaining. I was confident I could keep up with her and supply all of her wants and needs.

"Thank you," I responded as I took the glass from her and took a gulp of the sparkling pink wine.

"Did you have anything to do with Calico's death?" she inquired. "That nigga was found with a rat in his mouth, and his eyes were cut out. Everyone is in disbelief."

"Don't worry about it. Now that he's out of the way, I will take the throne and have you right by my side as my queen." I rubbed her cheek with my hand.

I thought back to the funeral that I'd gone to just to be nosy, and so that I didn't look suspect. Dressed in all black and my Dolce & Gabbana shades, I was playing the part to the hilt. Calico had plenty of people from near and far there to see him off. His mother, baby mamas, and thousands of "side-bitches" were all trying to hang on to the casket as the funeral groundskeepers lowered it into the ground. He had so many bitches there, for a minute I thought a fight was gonna break out.

"Like I said, Calico is gone. It's time for us to get on with our lives," I told her.

"Let's make a toast," Jewel suggested.

"To making money, happiness, and prosperity," I said, touching glasses with her.

"Well, I'll drink to that!" Jewel grinned then took a sip from her glass.

After she took several sips of her drink, she slowly took off her clothes, revealing a black lace teddy. She turned on the DVD player, and the song "12 Play" by R. Kelly came on. I had no idea how she knew this was one of my favorite songs. When she started dancing around and popping her ass in my face, my dick instantly got hard. One by one, she took off each piece of lingerie.

"You hungry?" she asked.

"A little."

Jewel began feeding me a little meat, cheese, and strawberries dipped in white chocolate.

"Now, I'm very hungry," she said before placing watermelon, cantaloupe, and honeydew melon all over my body.

Afterwards, she started eating it off me. I'd never had any girl do this shit to me. Before I knew it, she began licking my balls and deep-throating my dick. I closed my eyes. I couldn't help it and came right in her mouth. And she gladly swallowed.

"Damn!" I woke up with my dick covered in cum.

That was one of the best dreams I ever had. I took that as a sure sign that Jewel was going to be mine for good.

Chapter 8

"Snitch Bitch"

Sasha

"Free at last, free at last! Thank God Almighty, I'm free at last!" I loudly recited the famous words of Martin Luther King, Jr. as I exited the confines of Virginia Beach jail.

After spending three days there, a bitch was happy to finally get out. When I was originally booked on the lesser assault charge after speaking with the detectives, I went to speak to the magistrate about a bond. That bitch nigga denied me bond, claiming that I was a flight risk, since I lived out of state, so I had to wait to get a bond hearing. When I went before the judge, he granted me a $10,000 bond. I got in touch with a bondsman, and he let me out for a thousand dollars.

I waited patiently for my cab to arrive and literally jumped for joy when I saw him pull up.

"Yippee!" I skipped to the cab like a little kid and

hopped in the backseat. "The Doubletree Hotel at Military Circle Mall in Norfolk." I directed him to the hotel I'd stayed at during my arrest. I needed to return there to pick up my car.

As soon as the cabby pulled up to the hotel, I paid him, hopped into my car, and made my way to the interstate, headed back to Columbus, Georgia to my parents' crib to pick up my kids. I'd gotten my own little crib in Atlanta, but I rarely spent any time there.

As I was driving, the scene from New Year's Eve kept playing over and over in my head. The two things most disturbing to me were, one, I'd witnessed Touch getting shot by Calico, and two, I was so damn close to death myself. I knew in my heart that Calico would not have hesitated to put a bullet in me just as fast if he knew I was that chick that robbed him of his money. With that in mind, I began to reflect back on the agreement I'd made with Detective Tarver. *What the fuck have I done?* I wondered to myself, realizing I had made a big mistake. *I've just given myself a death sentence. Calico is gonna fucking kill me. I'm never gonna make it to court.*

My brain started racing, and my nerves were starting to get the better of me. If Calico found out I was an eyewitness, and planning to testify against him, he would make sure I didn't have a breath left in my body, come the trial date. As paranoia set in, I began constantly looking in my side-view and rearview mirrors to see if someone was following me. I was beginning to feel like a fucking lunatic fleeing from the crazy house.

For a moment I could have sworn that a tinted-out

black Tahoe was following me. I was so shook, my tank was on empty, but I refused to get gas. When I finally was forced, I circled the gas station two times to be sure no one was following me into the station. I pumped my gas and jumped back on the interstate in record-breaking time.

As I continued to drive, my brain was constantly plagued by this whole Calico situation, so I decided to give Detective Tarver a call.

"Tarver," he answered on the first ring.

"Hi, this is Sasha Williams. I just worked out a deal with you on that case involving the shooting at Club Encore in Virginia Beach."

"Hey, Sasha. What can I do for you?"

"Well, I was wondering if Calico would be informed that I will be testifying, because I'm a little worried about my safety."

"Well, we will inform him there is an eyewitness, but we won't reveal who until the court proceedings. But you don't have to worry. Once we get our hands on him, he will not be coming out, and until then, we will do all we can to make sure you're protected. Don't you worry."

"Okay," I said, still not feeling any more confident than I'd felt before the call. Actually, I felt worse.

I knew, after talking to the detective, there was no way I could go through with the deal we had negotiated. These days it was easier to beat the system than the streets. I could buck on court and be on the run and live to tell about it, as opposed to testifying against Calico and not even making it to court.

Now that I'd made my mind up that I wasn't going to court to testify against Calico, nor my charge for that matter, I had to put an escape plan into play. I knew it was nothing to change my look, get a new driver's license and relocate. I could easily go someplace like Jamaica and live with no problem. I knew a few people there. Plus, I would be in heaven, with so much Jamaican dick to choose from.

The only downfall would be leaving my family, baby daddy, and worst of all, my three- and seven-year-old sons, Malik and Jahad, whom I adored. I'm sure I could probably live without my sorry-ass drug-dealer-gone-bad baby daddy, Rick. Hell, he was part of the reason I had to resort to the streets.

I had actually stopped stripping at one point and was a working chick. I had a comfortable life, house, car, and even a rental property. Then this nigga's drug game got fucked up, and he drained me of every penny, leaving me with two foreclosed homes. And soon I was back to stripping and living with my parents. It wasn't until I bucked on Jewel for Calico's one hundred grand that I was able to get back on my feet. So that nigga, I could definitely do without, but it was the thought of being away from my kids that was killing me. Deep inside, I knew it would be too risky to have them with me while on the run.

My plan was set. I just needed to execute. I still had

about fifty grand left from Calico's money that I'd tricked Jewel into giving me, but I needed about fifty more. I wanted to have at least a hundred grand cash when I dipped out of the country. It was time for me to get my hustle on, and by all means I intended to. My life depended on it.

I called up my boy Diablo. Originally from Virginia, Diablo used to run drugs hard in VA but had recently moved to Atlanta when shit got hot, after a few young boys that he used as runners got locked up and started snitching. Although I didn't formally meet him until I started working at Bottoms Up, a strip club in Atlanta, I knew of him in VA because his name rang bells. And, of course, like every other baller, little miss Jewel used to date him too.

When Diablo hit the *A*, he started going even harder, making even more money, and eventually becoming one of the top suppliers in Atlanta. He used his drug money to open a club and started getting money from both angles.

"What up, sexy?" Diablo said.

"Hey, boo. I was calling to see if you were hiring," I said, knowing Diablo would know exactly what I meant. I'd done some work for him before, so he knew I was game for whatever.

"Not right now, baby girl. I'm waiting on some family to come up from out of the country. They should be here in a couple of weeks. Check with me then." Diablo spoke in code, saying that he was waiting for his product to come in.

"Cool," I said then ended the call.

The plan was set and soon to be in motion. I just needed to stay alive until then. I planned to use those couple of free weeks to spend time with my boys and let them know how much their mommy loved them, especially since, at this point, tomorrow definitely wasn't promised.

Chapter 9

"Nurse Save-a-chick"

Jewel

Touch had become more and more independent within the past weeks, so I was able to leave the house a little more often than when he first was discharged from the hospital. I was actually to the point of leaving him home alone. He enjoyed the independence of being left alone; it gave him a much-needed ego boost.

This particular day I'd chosen to take some time out for myself so I went to Starbucks. I was sitting in a booth there, sipping on a latte, using Starbucks Wi-Fi Connection on my laptop to look up some different wedding sites, and getting ideas about our wedding. It wasn't that we didn't have the Internet service or a computer at home. In fact, we had several, including the new HP TouchSmart PC. But I wanted to surprise Touch with how I set off our big date, so I didn't need him looking over my shoulders every minute while I was surfing the Web on our home computer.

I was planning on a major scale. I wanted a tailor-made Vera Wang dress, and a wedding setup to mimic a wedding of the royal court in England, with an aged mansion and horse and carriage to match. I'd even considered contacting David Tutera from the television show *My Fair Wedding* to guarantee that it would be a success. Our city wouldn't expect anything less than a celebrity wedding. Hell, we'd already set the tone with our New Year's party, so we had no choice but to continue the trend.

Although we hadn't set a date yet, I wanted our wedding to be the biggest event niggas in VA had ever seen, the wedding that would be talked about forever. I could already see the looks on the faces of all the haters when they see us stroll down the aisle. Our wedding was going to be the hottest shit VA had ever seen. We were definitely going down in history.

Although I'd plan to have an invitation-only event with police as security because there was no way Touch or I could take a chance of a replay from New Year's night, my guest list was already at five hundred. I was sure to invite all of the who's who and keep out all of the "who's you." I was on some presidential shit. I was even checking out some of the pictures of Obama's inauguration on the Internet, trying to get some additional ideas for entertainment, when I heard a familiar voice interrupt my concentration.

"Jewel, is that you? Hey, girl!"

I turned around in my booth and looked up from my laptop to see the nurse from the hospital, Misty. "Oh! Hey, Misty."

"How's your boo, Trayvon?" Misty used the same slang she'd used in the hospital the day we'd first met.

We both laughed, acknowledging that moment.

"He's great! He's walking without his walker now."

"Wonderful!"

"Misty, I just want to thank you for your kindness to us both while we were in the hospital." I reached out to shake her hand.

"That's my job." Misty flagged her hand in dismissal. "Damn, girl! Let me see that ring!" Seeing my unavoidable rock, she lifted my left hand. "Are you and Trayvon getting married?"

"Yes," I said, a Kool-Aid smile across my face. "We're engaged."

"Congratulations! Dang, that rock is heavy. And that diamond's almost blinding me. Whew! When's the big date?"

Before I could answer, my mouth flew wide open, and I put my hand over my heart. I gasped. I had seen Calico walk by the coffee shop in the shopping mall. I had heard he'd skipped town, and probably went back to Cali, but I knew this thing wasn't over between him and Touch. I was sure that was Calico, and I couldn't take any chances of him seeing me, so I ducked my head down in the booth where I sat.

"What's the matter?" Misty looked concerned.

"I think I just saw this dude, Calico."

"Who's Calico?"

"The guy who shot Touch."

"Oh my God. He hasn't been arrested yet?" Misty jumped in front of me in a protective manner as she scanned the area looking for Calico, and for a second, it looked like she was reaching for a gun on her hip.

"No," I said, kind of thrown by her demeanor.

"We better get out of here." Misty grabbed me by the arm. "Let's slip out the back door, and we can take my truck. I'm parked in the back. I'll bring you back to get your car later."

I lowered my head and tiptoed, with Misty blocking my body, as she walked behind me. She led me to a black Tahoe with dark tint. She opened the passenger door for me, and I scooted down into the front seat.

Misty climbed in on the driver's side and hit the gas pedal. "How about if we go to my place and kick it for a while?"

I was surprised at just how cool Misty was. Sure, at the hospital she seemed like a down-to-earth chick, but I never would have expected us to click so easily.

I examined her from head to toe. She was dressed in D&G jeans, sneakers, and light jacket to match. She had her hair pulled up in a curly ponytail. Based on her attire alone, I would have to say, she was my type of female. Even so, I was still skeptical.

Generally speaking, I didn't trust women, and especially after how Sasha stabbed me in the back. But since I was already in the truck with her and she'd practically saved me from Calico, I figured what the hell.

"That's cool. You stay near here?"

"Yeah, not too far."

And not too far was right because, after a few turns and ten minutes flat, we were pulling up to some new three-story town homes off Independence Boulevard.

"These are nice. I didn't even know they were back here," I said as we pulled into Misty's two-car garage.

"Yeah, they're new. It's not much, but it's a cozy little spot, for me alone." Misty walked in the basement of the house from the garage.

It was a huge room with a sitting area, bathroom, minibar, and another area set up with workout equipment. I followed her up the first set of steps where the living room, kitchen, and the master bedroom sat. Giving me a quick tour, she then led me up another set of steps, where another two bedrooms were.

"We can relax in the basement," Misty said as she took off her coat and got comfortable.

We walked back to the basement, and Misty flipped on the flat-screen television that resembled the exact one I had at home, and handed me the remote.

"Watch whatever you like," she said to me, and then headed to the bathroom.

I used that moment as an opportunity to call Poppo. I needed to know what was up with our little arrangement. That run-in earlier was a little too close for comfort.

I called Poppo's phone over and over again, but he didn't answer. Finally I decided to leave a voice message. "Man, what's the deal with Calico? I just saw that nigga at the mall," I said, trying my best to whisper. "Are you gon' do this shit or what? 'Cause, on the real, it's gonna get done with or without you. So you gonna be a player in the game or a fucking water boy?" I knew the exact words to say to get in his head.

After completing my message, I rushed off the phone as Misty walked in.

"Can I make you a drink? I don't know about you, but I need a little something to relax my nerves."

"Ummmm, do you have any wine?" I asked, to see what kind of level she was on.

"Sure. What would you like? White Zinfandel, Merlot, Pinot?"

"How about Moscato?" I said, knowing she probably never heard of it.

"Coming right up," Misty said, surprising the hell out of me.

Damn! I guess me and this bitch really can roll, I thought to myself, peeping her style.

After a few drinks we both were quite tipsy. We spent the next hour chatting like we were two old biddies.

"So, tell me, when is the big date? Are you aiming for this summer? If so, you only have a couple months to plan."

"Well, I'm working on that. I had a late summer date set, but the owners of the historic mansion I'm trying to book aren't working with me."

"For real? Girl, I got all kinds of hookups. Tell me what you trying to do. What wedding scene do you have in mind?"

I spent the next ten minutes telling Misty all about my fantasy wedding, detail by detail.

"Wow! That's sounds beautiful! Do you have a wedding planner?"

"Nope. I thought about contacting David Tutera though."

We both laughed.

"Girl, save your money. I got your back. Wedding planning is my thing. Any event planning for that matter. I used to work for a huge event planning company before I moved to VA. When I got here I had my own company for a while. Then I got so involved in nursing, I let it go."

"Oh my God! What a blessing. I would love to have you be my wedding planner. It must have been meant for us to meet."

"That's destiny."

Misty and I tapped wineglasses as if we were giving a toast and took another gulp of wine.

Chapter 10

"Bitch Nigga"

Poppo

After I dropped Calico off at Norfolk International Airport, I checked my voicemail. Jewel had called me earlier, but I didn't want to answer, with Calico in my presence. I was sure she'd left a message.

"Are you gon' do this shit or what? 'Cause, on the real, it's gonna get done with or without you. So you gonna be a player in the game or a fucking water boy?"

I took the phone from my ear and looked at it. Listening to her message really pissed me off. It was like even this chick was taking me for a bitch. I wondered if I had the word *bitch* written on my fucking forehead, or if that shit Calico had was contagious.

I called Jewel back. My first instinct was to let that little bitch have it, but instead I decided to hear her out.

"Poppo, what the fuck is going on?" she said as soon

as she picked up the phone. "You bitching up on me or what?"

Fuck this! This bitch got me fucked up. Without saying a word, I straight hung up on her ass, not thinking twice about it. I thought I had the patience to tolerate the little attitude she was giving, but I guess I didn't.

Ring! Ring!

When Jewel called right back, I put her in her place this time. "Yo," I answered the phone, "you gon' have to bring that shit down a few notches, ma."

"I'm saying . . . I thought we had a deal?"

"Jewel, I'm a man of my word. I got you, baby girl. This shit takes planning. Calm the fuck down. Have a drink or something. Let me do my shit. I gotta do it where there is no repercussions. But if this nigga makes you nervous, then you will be happy to know Calico is on his way back to California. He was only in VA to look for this bitch Sasha."

"Sasha? What he want with her? Don't tell me he dealing with that sheisty bitch!" Jewel snapped.

"Nah, ma, not at all. That nigga want to deal with her on some whole other shit." Then I suggested, "Why don't we meet up? I don't really do the phone thing."

"Okay. I feel you. What about that little Mexican spot off of Newtown and Virginia Beach Boulevard."

Jewel picked a real inconspicuous spot. For sure no one would have ever seen us up there.

"Cool. Meet you there in about an hour," I told her. "When I see you, I'll get you up to speed on everything."

"A'ight." Jewel hung up the phone.

I had decided to meet up with Jewel not only because I wasn't into the phone thing, but I needed to see her face to face so I could read her. Deep inside, I still didn't quite trust that bitch, so I was proceeding with caution.

I knew exactly what my plans were. I was gonna use Sasha to lure Calico to Atlanta, and once I got him there, I was gonna let him have it. I needed to get that nigga in an unfamiliar area. A place where I knew he had no alliance. That would make my job all the easier. I had shit all mapped out, but I was planning to tell Jewel as little as possible, at least until I felt I could trust her a little more.

After leaving the airport, I made a quick stop by Mo Dean's to pick up a few dollars from Murdock, a nigga that owed me money from a little business we'd arranged a few days earlier. I spotted his car as soon as I pulled into the parking lot. Luckily he was sitting in his car when I pulled up. I parked right next to him. I wanted to get shit done quick so I could shoot up the boulevard and meet up with Jewel.

"What up, man?" I said through the car window.

"Ain't shit."

Murdock got out of his car, and I unlocked the doors so he could hop in mine.

"Here you go." He handed me a wad of money with rubber bands separating them.

"What's this?" I always asked niggas how much they were giving me off the jump, to prevent any confusion.

"Five grand for now?"

"Five grand for now? When am I gonna see the other ten?" I asked, a little aggravated that Murdock didn't have all of my loot.

"I got you, Poppo. I just need a little while longer."

"Yeah, okay, nigga." I placed the money in the glove box then locked it. "Do I need to count after you?" I asked, even though I was gonna count the money, regardless of what Murdock said.

"It's all there, man. Have I ever shorted you before, muthafucka?"

"Nah, nigga. You know better than that. Now get out my car. I got shit to do. Gotta make this paper!"

"Gone!"

Murdock hopped out of my car, and I began to back out of the parking spot. I watched as he walked up to the barbershop next to Mo Dean's and started talking to a couple of guys that stood out front. By the time I reached the end of the parking lot, the police was flooding the place. I busted a right turn onto Virginia Beach Boulevard and never looked back.

"Whew!" I let out a deep breath. I'd just made it. I ain't have shit on me but I wasn't trying to be in that fucking mix up. I turned up the radio and relaxed as I passed Booker T. Washington High School.

Werp! Werp!

No sooner than I thought I was safe from danger, I heard sirens behind me. "Gotdamn!" I said to no one in particular. I pulled over and waited for the officer to come to the car. I watched from my side- and rearview mirrors as he walked up. Then I rolled down my window.

"License and registration please."

"Can I ask why you pulled me over?" I asked as I gave the officer the information he'd asked for.

"I've been following you for some time. I got behind you after you pulled out of the shopping center on Church Street. You were swerving. Have you been drinking today, sir?"

"Yeah, right." I laughed. I knew everything this cop was saying was bullshit. He just needed a reason to pull me over.

"Well, you don't seem drunk, and I don't smell any alcohol, but let me run your license. If everything comes back okay, I'll send you off with a warning."

"Yes, sir," I said, just trying to cooperate. It's when cats act all nervous or aggressive that cops harass their ass even more. I waited and waited for the officer to come back.

After about five minutes he walked back to the car. He had his right hand on his cuffs. After seeing that, I already knew what time it was.

"Could you step out of the car please?"

That was my confirmation. This nigga was about to take me to jail. "What am I being arrested for?" I asked as I stepped out of the car.

"Driving on a suspended license?"

"What?" I asked, knowing what this nigga was saying couldn't be true.

"You had a ticket a few months back that you never paid. It resulted in your license being suspended."

"Nah, man. I paid that," I explained. "I got the receipt in my wallet."

"Save the excuses for the magistrate, man. Watch your head." The officer put me in the backseat of his car.

I was pissed off as I took a quick ride down the street and around the corner to Norfolk City jail. This was truly some bullshit. I had paid that damn ticket and even had the receipt to prove it, and I still was going to jail on a damn suspended license.

When we drove through the gates, the officer escorted me inside the jail and sat me in the holding tank. I sat there patiently as I waited to speak to the magistrate. I shook my head in disgust as I looked at the drunk that sat beside me covered in vomit and piss. Then I glanced over at the prostitute that sat on the bench across from me, smacking on her gum like it was the last piece of Bubblicious on earth. She stared me in the face, constantly giving me the eye. I watched as the people who were getting released walked past me and out the back door. I could only wish I was in their shoes.

"Terrell Johnson," an officer called out to me.

"Yes."

"Right this way, man."

I followed the officer to fingerprinting. Five minutes later my picture had been taken, and I was done with fingerprinting.

I had to see the magistrate next. As I sat waiting on

him, I could see his office from the window. Through the crack of the door, I could see some fine-ass chick standing, her hair pulled up in a curly ponytail. She had that good hair, the kind that curled up when it got wet. She was dressed in D&G jeans that was tight to death and gripped her plump ass just right.

Minutes later, she was no longer in sight, and the magistrate was walking into the room. As soon as he was settled in front of me, I explained my situation. I told him that I'd paid my ticket and had the receipt to prove it. Come to find out, the reason my shit was suspended was because, after I paid the ticket to the court clerk, I was supposed to take the receipt to DMV and get my license reinstated. Lucky for me, the magistrate had mercy, and he let me out on a personal release bond, where no bondsman was needed, just my signature saying I will appear in court.

Thirty minutes later, I was one of those people getting released that I'd admired earlier.

I sat outside the precinct waiting on a cab so I could go pick my car up from the pound. Just my luck, the same chick I'd seen earlier came strolling out the precinct door.

"Hey, beautiful." I couldn't let her pass by without saying a word.

"What's up?"

"What's a woman like you doing in a place like this?"

"Handling business. But I'm sure I could guess what a thug like you is doing in a place like this. Your second home, I bet."

That bitch had just gone from beautiful to beast. At that time I realized what they said about a person being pretty until they open their mouth was true.

"You know what, ma . . . I'm not gonna even entertain that bullshit. You have a nice day." I walked away when I noticed my cab had arrived.

Chapter 11

"Always on the Grind"

Sasha

I'd managed to lay low and lived to see another two weeks. Eager to get on my grind, I called Diablo up to see if he was ready for me to work.

Like clockwork, his package had arrived, and he had work for me. I wasted no time dropping my kids off at my parents' house, kissing them good-bye, and hopping on the interstate and heading back to Atlanta.

After an hour of driving, I arrived at Crossroads Bar and Grill, Diablo's newly opened sports bar. Although he wasn't open for business when I arrived, I walked in to see a pretty busy atmosphere. Knowing I was wanted on the streets, I was a little paranoid when walking in.

I immediately located Diablo, and we took a seat in a booth in the corner, from where I had a clear view of everything in the club. Even though there were groups of guys gathered about in different areas, I took a few moments to check out each of them.

First, I scanned a group of guys gambling in one section of the club. None of them looked familiar. Next, I checked out a group that played a game on the PlayStation 3 and none of them looked suspect.

Finally, feeling comfortable, I directed my attention toward Diablo. I asked him, "So what's the deal?"

He told me, "Well, I got a few deliveries you can take care of for me—one in Florida, the other in Alabama, and the last just around the corner in Fort Valley."

"Oh, I got you. All those are around the corner for me. You know I got you."

"Cool. So we'll set you up for Alabama first."

"A'ight," I said, anxious to get my hands on my first little piece of dough, "I'm ready now."

"A'ight den. Let's do this. Drive around to the back of the club."

I did just as Diablo had instructed and drove to the back.

Diablo brought out the packages of cocaine and told me to stand back. I almost fainted as I watched him take off the door panel of my new car. I knew he had to hide the shit in a secure area, but just seeing the door panel off my car like that fucked me up.

Oh, well, it's all part of the game. It'll be well worth it in the end, I thought as I looked on.

I knew in the end everything would end in my favor. That's one thing I always made sure of. My motto was, why settle for milk when you can have the cow? Just like that shit with Jewel—sure, she was a good friend and she looked out for a bitch—but why would I keep waiting for a handout, when I could easily take hers and do my own thing?

Chapter 12

"Back on the Scene"

Touch

"Hey, Touch. What's good witcha?"

"Man, you looking a'ight. Can't even tell a nigga got shot."

"Long time no see, big homie."

Everybody dapped me up as I stepped on the scene.

Just as I'd done when standing on my throne at Club Encore New Year's night, I held both of my hands in the air in a kingly fashion. "Yeah, y'all niggas know what time it is. The king is back."

I had just walked in "A New Look," a barbershop where all the ballers and street niggas went to get their hair cut. Behind the barbershop was another room with a pool table and a crap table, where men came to smoke weed, brag and talk shit, and lie about all the money they had and bitches they fucked. The truth be known, more business transactions took place there than corporate America handled on the golf course.

The spot was packed, which made my entrance all the more dramatic. The whole barbershop atmosphere made a nigga feel real dapper, just from the smell of after-shave and powder, the sound of clippers, and rap music that played in the background. This was a man's thing. Nothing like a fresh cut and shave to make a man feel like a man. I was already jiggy with my gear and an added fresh cut was exactly what I needed to make me feel like my old self. I hopped in Mike's chair and requested my usual "edge-up." I wanted and needed to feel like "that nigga" again.

This was the first time I'd been out since my recovery. I was determined to go back in public holding my head high, to let niggas know I wasn't scared of the streets. Sure, I'd gotten shot, but I wasn't letting that shit hold me down. I was strapped with my Glock and dressed in the best. Although I only wore a pair of Robin's jeans, a plain beige D&G thermal shirt, and a fresh pair of wheat Timberlands, it was the Louis Vuitton scarf and skullcap that really set it off. I was finally walking with no assistance, free from walker and cane, so I was feel-ing on top of the world.

As Mike prepared to line me up, everyone gathered around me to shout me out and sincerely seemed happy to see me. They acted like I was Lazarus being resurrected from the dead, which, in a sense, I was, or better yet, like I was some return war hero from Iraq.

These streets were at war, and that ain't no joke. I could have died, fucking with that damn Calico, and I'd planned to dead that nigga as soon as I located his snake ass.

When I finished getting my cut, a few niggas gave me pounds, tapped shoulders, did the infamous handshake that all street cats do.

Raz, another heavy drug nigga on the streets, called out, "Hey, I heard you and Jewel gon' tie that knot."

"Yeah, we decided to do that thang," I said, acting nonchalant.

"Word on the streets is, Jewel got a diamond on her finger so big, it's making bitches sick!" Mike said.

"Yeah, sort of like mine." I gave them a glimpse of the ice I was holding.

"Y'all niggas doing it . . . living large," Raz chimed back in.

"What you mean, nigga? I'm trying to be like you," I said jokingly to Raz.

Suddenly the shop was filled with boisterous sounds of admiration and compliments. Everyone stood around and examined my platinum wedding band with my engraved initials boldly lifted across the band. Jewel had picked this ring out to match hers, which was just as large.

"Man, that ring is sick!"

"Damn, nigga! I ain't never seen no ring like that."

The dick riders started to add their praises.

"Hey, my lady says y'all niggas gon' put on the wedding of the century. They say Barack Obama and

Michelle's inauguration ain't gon' have nothing on y'all thang. We got our invitation the other day."

This started a round of everyone saying they did or didn't get their invitation.

I held up my hands good-naturedly. "Hold up. I'll make sure Jewel get y'all niggas your invitation. If you don't get one, on the real, everyone here today is officially invited," I said, knowing Jewel would have a fucking fit if she knew I invited everyone from the barbershop. Knowing her, she didn't send them an invite on purpose.

I finally felt like I was in my element again. I was back, back on center stage where I belonged. All of a sudden, the room fell quiet. I was still popping shit with one of my niggas when I heard somebody whisper, "Poppo's here."

I looked up to see that bitch-ass nigga standing in the door, staring at me. In one quick motion, I went for my Glock, which was in the holster hooked on my belt. My first instinct was to kill his bitch ass, but I knew I was in a public place, filled with snitches. I knew wherever Poppo was, Calico wasn't too far away. I threw my left hand in the air as to say, "What's up?" I didn't want to have to light the barbershop up, but I would, if I had to.

To my surprise, Poppo threw both hands up in the air on some white-flag, I-surrender shit, letting me know he wasn't trying to beef, at least not at that point. I didn't trust that nigga as far as I could see his scandalous ass, though.

"Hey, nigga, you need to relax. Just consider me your savior," Poppo said in a low tone as he passed me.

Everyone's eyes beamed on that nigga Poppo, their ears almost peeled back. Poppo looked just like one of those 2Pac-ass West Side muthafuckas too, dressed in Converse, jeans, and a flannel shirt. This cat was a fucking joke.

"Nigga, what is you talking about?" I screwed my faced up and wondered how his bitch ass could ever be my savior.

"Ask your bitch."

I could feel my temper rising. "What the fuck you say?" I started to rush his ass, but everyone grabbed me and held me back.

Poppo looked at me and said, "I ain't got no beef with you, little homie. Just ask your old lady what it is." With that, he left.

Although I stayed and let the African broad in the shop braid my hair, my mind was churning, and I was burning up inside. *Ain't life a bitch? I almost got killed, my wifey stands by me, then the next thing I know, that bitch is trying to do me.*

Chapter 13

"The Run-in"

Poppo

I walked out the barbershop wondering if I'd just fucked things up. It was bad enough I had missed my meeting with Jewel when I'd gotten arrested, and I hadn't heard from her since. Then I get into a fucking argument with Touch. I probably shouldn't have said shit about nothing, but that shit just came out of nowhere. I never expected to run into that nigga, Touch. Then it was how this nigga came at me. What the fuck was I suppose to do? Bitch up? Nah, I wasn't about to let that shit happen. But I should have been a little smarter about how I handled shit 'cause, if Touch didn't know about the plan, for sure it was gonna bring problems between him and his bitch. I was expecting a call from Jewel soon enough.

Ring! Ring!

My phone rang sooner than I'd expected. I thought

73

it was Jewel. I looked down at my phone. To my surprise it was Murdock.

"What up, nigga? You ready for me?" I said, hoping this nigga had my ten grand.

I'd been waiting some time for my dough, and a nigga was getting restless. For a minute I thought he had bucked on me for my money. I had actually called that nigga a few times and left a couple of threatening messages. Sometimes that's what it took to get a reaction out of a nigga.

"I got a little something for you, man. You can come check me at the Caribbean spot."

"I'm on my way."

It took no time for me to arrive at our usual spot, Mo Dean's. I walked in the restaurant to find Murdock sitting at the bar.

"What up, duke?" I dapped him up.

"Can I get you a drink?" Murdock offered.

"Nah, man. I ain't here for that. Let me get that off of ya, so I can get out of here. You know I don't like hanging around out here. This spot getting hot. I got locked up on some bullshit the last time I was out here fucking with you."

"Yeah, man. The fucking police flooded the joint as soon as you left that day. They had niggas lined up on the wall, searching cats and running IDs. I was lucky though; everything with me was straight. A couple of niggas got locked up for possession, and a few niggas had warrants."

"Damn! That's fucked up. So what you got for me?" I asked, getting back to business.

"Fifteen."

"Fifteen? You only owe me ten. Did you forget you already paid me five? As much as I would love to take your money, I won't do that to you."

"Nah, fifteen hundred." Murdock handed me the small stack of money.

"Fifteen hundred? What the fuck is really going on, Murdock? You trying to play a nigga or what? I feel like you trying to play me." My patience was running thin with Murdock. He'd been holding on to my money way too long now.

"Come on, Poppo. Man, you know I would never try to play you. We ain't never had no problem with money. Trust me, Poppo, I got you, man."

"You said that same shit the last time we met up. I can't keep hearing the same bullshit. You got one week, nigga. Rob somebody. Fuck it! Rob a bank! But do what the fuck you gotta do to get me my fucking dough." I put the little change Murdock gave me in my pocket then walked away.

Days passed and I ain't hear from Jewel about my little run-in with Touch, so I figured shit was as usual. And I wasn't about to call her so she could tell me something different, 'cause once I went through with the shit, she couldn't renege on the deal. Or, in turn, I would have to deal with her and her bitch nigga too.

So Calico was on his way to Atlanta, and like always, I

was on my way to the airport to pick him up. But this time I didn't mind, because I knew this would be the last time. I'd spent years flying here and driving there to deliver packages and pick up money while he sat in California and collected the money off of all my hard work, sweat, and blood. Hell, I had a crib, family, and baby mother in Cali that I wanted to spend time with too. Instead, I was always on the road for that nigga, hopping from telly (hotel) to telly, living out of a fucking suitcase.

I spotted Calico as soon as I bent the corner. Like a proud chauffeur, I pulled up with a smile on my face, trying not to show one sign of deceit on my face.

Chapter 14

"Fucked-up Luck"

Calico

I'd never been so happy to get the fuck off a plane in my life. Hours on a plane from Los Angeles to Atlanta with crying babies, stinking-ass niggas, and no weed was straight fucking torture. As soon as I exited the airport and hopped in the car with Poppo, I sparked up the "kush." I took in one deep pull and let it marinate then let it out slowly. Almost instantly a nigga was relaxed.

"What up, duke?" Poppo greeted me as soon as I got in the car.

"You, nigga. You fucking slipping. You got a nigga on the road and shit when you know a nigga wanted. I'm trying to fucking lay low."

"Speaking of wanted, how the fuck you fly anyway?"

"I flew as Thomas Jones, nigga. I used a fake ID. You know you can buy those a dime a dozen in the hood."

77

"I knew you had something up your sleeve."

"Nuff of that shit. Where we headed, nigga? And you got yo' heat?" I asked right away, never really trusting Poppo.

He was the reason I was forced to take a trip to Atlanta anyway. This nigga had been slipping lately. I couldn't understand why so many days had passed and this bitch Sasha was still breathing. And when I questioned this nigga about it, he had all kinds of excuses. It wasn't until I threatened to kick his ass that he started acting like he had some damn sense. He'd heard from one of his boys that Sasha was working for his man, Diablo. On top of that, Diablo was about his paper and was looking for a West Coast connection, so he was definitely a nigga I needed to holla at. I figured I could kill two birds with one stone—befriend this nigga, make some money, and set up an easy kill for Sasha's snake ass.

"I gotta make a stop. Then after that we headed straight to Diablo's spot." Poppo handed me the gun from his waist.

We drove for about fifteen minutes. Then I noticed we were in a rough area. We were obviously in the hood. Niggas were walking around with oversized white tees, jeans to their knees, do-rags and fitted caps. Everybody looked fucking suspect, like they were just looking for trouble. Being that I was on the run, I knew this wasn't the place for me. I was sure the police lived in areas like this hood.

"Where the fuck we at, nigga?" I asked, not feeling too secure with my surroundings.

"Bankhead. Don't worry, this shit will be real quick."

Poppo pulled up to a set of rundown apartments and jumped out the car.

"A'ight, nigga. Just hurry the fuck up." I pulled out the gun that he had given me earlier from my waist and put one bullet in the head.

I constantly monitored my surroundings as I waited for Poppo to come back. I couldn't take the chance of being caught up in some bullshit. I pulled out my cell to check the time and noticed I had a missed call from my baby mother.

One complete minute hadn't passed before the car door opened and I was face to face with a dope fiend carrying a butcher knife.

"Give me your fucking money!" he demanded.

Almost instantaneously, like a reflex, I lifted my gun and pulled the trigger. *Click!*

Nothing. The fucking gun had jammed on me. I knew this was do-or-die, so my mind went straight into survivor mode.

Bam! I busted the fiend in the head with the butt of the gun, knocking him to the ground.

Just then Poppo walked up. "What the fuck is going on, man?"

"Nothing, nigga. Your piece-of-shit gun almost got me killed. That's all."

"What you mean?"

"Just get me the fuck out of here!" I said, pissed the fuck off.

Poppo hit the gas, and we skidded off.

I exhaled and shook my head as I thought about things as we drove toward the interstate. *I knew this neighborhood was bad luck.* Relieved that I'd escaped without injury or jail, I relaxed and unjammed Poppo's little bullshit gun and placed it snug in my waist.

Minutes later, we pulled up to Crossroads Bar and Grill. Although the club was closed, it was still niggas everywhere, cats in one corner playing Madden on the projector screen, another set of cats gambling in the next corner, and the owner, Diablo, in another spot having what looked like a serious conversation with another cat.

Always willing to take a gamble, I immediately started watching the dice game. It looked like Diablo was gonna be busy for a minute, so I decided to get in on the game.

My luck was running good, and I was killing those country-ass A-town niggas when Poppo came over and interrupted the game.

"Diablo, ready to holla at you, man."

With that, I grabbed up my money and walked away. I counted my money as I walked toward Diablo. I'd won fifteen hundred dollars in that little bit of time.

Poppo introduced us, and I carried the conversation from there. There was no need for a bunch of talking. It was understood niggas was there to make money.

"Look, my shit is on point. I can get however much coke you need. I get my shit from across the border, so it's top-notch. I been bringing this shit over from the West Coast to the East Coast for years, and I had VA on lock, so I know can't nobody else make you a better offer." I continued by telling my numbers.

After a short negotiation, we had an agreement. The deal was set, and it was time for me to get the fuck out of dodge. I instructed Poppo to get me to my hotel. A nigga was wanted, and I wasn't trying to spend too much time on the streets.

Minutes later Poppo pulled up to a hotel right off the interstate on La Vista Road. He went in and reserved the room then came back.

"Room one twenty-four," he said and handed me the card key.

I grabbed my bags and went straight to my room. Once in the room, I kicked off my shoes, laid my piece-of-shit gun on the nightstand, and laid across the bed with remote in one hand and dick in the other as I began to flip through the television channels. Moments later, I began to drift off to sleep.

What seemed like no more than thirty minutes into my nap, a hunger pang hit my belly like a right hook. I woke up, grabbed the guest book, and flipped through the pages to see what nearby restaurants delivered. I chose to go with pizza.

I decided to roll a joint while I was waiting for my pizza. I pulled out my deodorant and rolled it until the bar was completely out. Beneath it was a quarter of kush. Then I searched my bag for Backwoods to roll it with.

"Fuck!" I yelled out loud.

I was experiencing a weed smoker's worst nightmare. I had weed and no fucking paper to roll it with. For a second I considered ripping a few pages from the Bible to roll up, but something inside of me just wouldn't let that happen. With the shit I was in, I needed the Lord on my side, so I couldn't take the risk of disrespecting His Holy Word. I could possibly wait until the pizza arrived to smoke, but I knew after I ate I would definitely have to smoke. It was like dessert after dinner.

I called up Poppo. That nigga had to come back and take me to the store or bring me some Backwoods or something.

"Yo!"

I was relieved Poppo answered his phone right away. "Poppo, where you at?"

"Across town. What's up?"

"Man, I need some Backwoods bad."

"A'ight, I got you. Give me about thirty minutes."

Poppo said exactly what I wanted to hear.

Remembering my baby mother had called earlier, I called Cali to talk to my kids as a way to pass time. And that's exactly what happened. I was so wrapped up in my conversation with my four kids and two baby mothers, I didn't even realize forty-five minutes had passed.

As soon as I hung up the phone with them and was about to call Poppo, the pizza arrived. Feeling hungry as a hostage, I decided to eat first and then call Poppo after.

Once my belly was full, I called Poppo, and the phone went straight to voicemail. It didn't even ring. I hung up and called right back. I got the same thing. I tried two more times, and each time I got straight voicemail.

"Fuck it!"

Fed up, I put on my shoes, and grabbed a few dollars. I was trying to lay low and not show my face too much because I was in Atlanta to do Sasha in. Plus, I had that outstanding warrant. But a nigga would straight lose his mind without weed, so I headed out of the hotel and to a little corner store I saw at the end of the street.

I was excited to see exactly what I needed behind the counter as soon as I walked in. I stood in line at the busy store, anxious to get my papers and get back to my hotel room. For three minutes I'd stood in line, and it hadn't moved at all. For a minute, I thought about leaving and going to the gas station across the street, but I figured I may as well stay, since I was already here.

I looked down at my vibrating phone. It was Poppo calling. I wasn't even trying to talk to that fool at this point. I pressed *ignore*, sending him to voicemail. Finally, the line started to move and minutes later I was at the counter paying for my Backwoods to roll up my weed. As I reached for my change and bag, I heard a commotion at the front door.

"Don't move! Everybody, down. Get on the fucking ground!"

Narcotic police agents had flooded the place.

Muthafuckas, I thought to myself as I lay on the ground. Running wasn't even an option. I was surprised when the cops ran right past me and to the back of the store then started bringing out the workers in cuffs, while another officer cuffed each of the customers, searched us, and ran our identification.

How bad can a nigga's luck be? Talk about wrong place at the wrong time. I had, just by chance, walked into a store that was a known drug spot. I felt confident I would be walking out though. Once again the fake ID had come in handy. One by one the officers had begun to release the customers that had no drugs on them and whose names had come back clear.

One of the officers approached me. "Can I get your ID?"

I searched every pocket for my wallet. *Fuck!* I thought to myself in a panic. I had left my wallet in the hotel room.

"No ID?" the officer asked, noticing my frustration.

"Nah, man. I can give you my name, date of birth, and social, though," I said, knowing I had the information from my fake ID memorized.

I ran off the information to the officer as if it was my own. He jotted it down and went back to his car to run a check. I waited patiently with a few others, as another cop watched over us.

Minutes later, the first officer returned. "Mr. Jones," he called out to me, while pulling out his handcuffs.

What the fuck! I wondered what the hell was going on.

I didn't respond, I just looked at him with face of confusion.

"We're gonna have to take you in, son. You have an outstanding warrant out for nonpayment of child support."

I be damn! I knew I should have stayed my black ass in Cali. There is no way one man's luck could be so fucked up! I already knew what was in store for me. Once I got to the jail, they would run my fingerprints and find out who I really was. From there, I would be extradited to VA. My shit was fucked up. I was going straight to jail without a get-out-of-jail-free card.

Chapter 15

"The Wedding's Off"

Touch

When I'd gotten home from the barbershop, I'd planned to let Jewel's conniving ass have it. But the rational side of me just couldn't allow that to happen so quickly. It took all I had, but I went on with the days as usual while I decided on the best way to approach things.

I was the type of nigga that liked to have all my ducks in a row, so when I came with it, I came hard. I liked to be confident that it wasn't shit a bitch or nigga could say to lie their way out of things. I knew I was about to make a hell of an allegation, so I wanted to be sure I had my facts straight when I did it.

After running that day at the barbershop through my head over and over, along with all the other shit that had happened during New Year's, I was sure that bitch was on some sheisty shit. My fucking blood was boiling as I waited patiently for her to come in from the beauty salon.

When she got home, she rushed up to me all kissy-poo and shit. She was wearing leggings, a fitted sweater dress that grabbed tight to every curve of her perfect body, and was smelling of my favorite perfume, Viktor & Rolf Flowerbomb. I had to admit, that shit was quite tempting, but that alone wasn't gonna work this day. I had to give it to her though. She was a good actress. She could've won a fucking Academy Award for the act she put on, and she could have really fooled an amateur, but I wasn't buying the bullshit she was selling.

Before I could dig into her ass, I noticed she had some broad with her. I rolled my eyes at this woman, but Jewel didn't seem to pay me any attention. "Who is this?" I grunted, glaring at her new woman friend. I thought Jewel would have learned her lesson with Sasha.

"Oh, baby, this is Misty. Don't you remember? She's the nurse who took care of us when we were in the hospital. And, lo and behold, she does freelance wedding planning on the side. I hired her as our wedding planner."

"We don't need a wedding planner," I mumbled.

Misty must have picked up my bad mood, because she grabbed her oversized Chanel bag and stepped toward the door. "Well, I'll see you, Jewel. We'll talk later."

"Okay, Misty." Jewel walked her to the door and waved to her.

"Bye, Jewel. Talk to you soon."

Jewel turned back to me like nothing was wrong and said, "Baby, come check out my bridesmaids' colors.

They're going to wear lavender. I don't want no loud, ghetto-looking colors. Yeah, baby, this wedding is gonna have class all the way."

I followed Jewel to her computer room, where she had all the latest bridal magazines spread out on the floor, an indication that she had gone too far. Plus, she'd hired a damn wedding planner. I didn't even think she knew all this stuff, but obviously, Miss Bourgeois Virginia Beach Bitch knew her shit, when it came to wedding time.

And worse still, she knew money wasn't coming in like regular. I'd been laid up for a few months now, so I hadn't been doing no work. And the last count I had, this broad had spent about fifty thousand on the wedding, and we ain't even walked down the fucking aisle. Just thinking about it made steam come out my ears.

"And baby, we're gonna have orchids and baby's breath." Suddenly, Jewel looked up, as if for the first time she had tuned into my sour mood.

"Baby, what's the matter?" she asked, her face twisted into a corkscrew of concern.

This made me all the madder, that she could sound so innocent. *Yeah, right, bitch!* "You know what's the matter." I grabbed her by the neck and looked her in the eye.

She looked all surprised and shit. "No, I don't, baby. What is it? I ain't no mind reader."

"I can't believe you'd do me like this, Jewel."

"What are you talking about?"

"I'm out at the barbershop and this nigga Poppo talking shit to me, like you and him running game together."

"What the hell are you talking about, Touch?"

"So you fucking that nigga now?"

"What? I'm with you every day. I sleep with you every single night. So how the hell do I have time to be fucking somebody else?"

"Well, you gon' tell me something. How is this nigga talking about he gon' be my savior?"

"How the hell am I supposed to know what that nigga was talking about? You know he ain't nothing but Calico's little bitch. You can't believe nothing he says."

"Yeah, I should have never fucked with you in the first place. You the one who was Calico's bitch."

"How you gon' throw that in my face, Touch? Did you forget I made us? I'm the reason we have this house, the cars, the lifestyle of the ghetto fabulous. It was my money from ghostwriting and my connect with TMF that got us here! Oh- and who took care of you when you were sick? I even washed your ass for you and wiped it when you had to shit."

"Oh, just a regular Florence Nightingale. I knew you was gone throw that shit up in my face. But, bitch, you didn't have to do nothing for me."

"Nah, I'm much more than a night nurse. Just so that you know, I was hollering at Poppo to save your ass! I promised to put him on if he took care of Calico for you."

"What the fuck I look like to you? You must take me for some little bitch. You really got me fucked up. Do your thing, Jewel. I'm out." I grabbed my keys, walked out the front door, and never looked back.

I was fuming as I drove. I didn't know where I was headed, but I knew I needed to get the fuck away from Jewel. I wondered what type of cat she took me for. *Do I look like some type of weak nigga that need protection?* My weeks of rehab must have fucked her head up. That broad was tripping.

Finally cooling off a little bit I decided to go to one of my old spots, Mo Dean's Caribbean restaurant and lounge. As soon as I walked in, I felt right at home. The atmosphere hadn't changed a bit.

My boy Raz spotted me as soon as I walked in. "Touch, what up, nigga!"

"Ain't shit, nigga." I headed straight to the bar.

I hadn't been sitting a whole minute before I felt someone hug me from behind and caress my manhood. Off the jump, I knew exactly who that was. It was only one chick that came on hard like that, Dirty Diana.

"What up, baby girl?" I spun around on the barstool to face her.

"Looks like you," she said, referencing my standing dick.

"So what you gon' do about it?" I said, knowing exactly how she got down.

"Oh, you know the deal. I ain't trying to hurt you though. I heard you got shot. Everything healed up okay? You know I puts it down, and I don't want to be responsible for no injuries." She giggled.

"I'm strong and long as a horse." I pulled Diana between my legs and squeezed her ass tight, all the while reminiscing about the last time I fucked her.

Diana was a jump-off bitch that I'd fucked one night on a whim. I knew her face from the spot, but I never really paid her much attention. Hell, I ain't even know her name until the night I fucked her. Her body was tight, and the fuck was good, but every nigga with a little dough had ran up in that. I remember when I fucked her. She was on point, but as soon as we were done, that bitch had her fucking hand out for money. Needless to say, I gave it to her, and I would do it again too. Sad to say, but the fuck was definitely worth it.

Damn! Times were good before I hooked up with Jewel and got locked down. What the fuck was I thinking when I asked her to marry me? I was still gripping Diana's firm ass tight.

"Well, you know I'm working, so as soon as I get off—"

"Say no more." I cut her off mid-sentence, noticing my baby mother, Ciara, staring at me from the cut.

Although I missed my kids like crazy and wanted badly to see them, I wasn't trying to see that bitch. That last time I saw her, I had beat the shit out of her and ended up in jail. She, just like Jewel, just had to fuck Calico.

I turned back around to the bar, pretending to not even see her. If it wasn't for my pending case and the temporary restraining order she had on me, I would have gone over there and beat her ass again. There was no amount of beating that could be punishment enough for the line that bitch had crossed.

"Let me get a Grey Goose on the rocks."

"That's on me," one of my boys told the bartender. "Put all his drinks on my tab."

I spent the next hour, kicking it with my niggas and drinking Grey Goose like it was water. Before I knew it, I was fucked up.

"Yo, I'm out, niggas," I said to my boys as I scrambled to get off of my barstool.

"Hold on, nigga. We can't let you drive like that. You just got out the hospital from one injury. We can't send you right back."

"Oh, he straight," I heard a familiar female voice say.

I looked up to see my ex-girlfriend, Lisa. Ghetto spots like Mo Dean's wasn't her thing. "What you doing here?"

"Don't you worry about it. Just be happy I'm here and willing to help your drunk ass," she said, escorting me out the door.

I looked back to see Diana giving me a dirty look. Sure, I wanted to fuck that, but Lisa had taken over. Besides, I knew Diana was guaranteed pussy. I could hit that at any day any time. I was lucky to get an opportunity to get up in Lisa's stuff again because we'd broken up on bad terms. I was even surprised she had approached a nigga.

"Where did you park?"

"That way." I pointed.

Minutes later we were in my car.

"Where to?" Lisa asked.

"To my crib. Don't act like you don't know the way. You used to live there, remember?" I said, thinking back to the times Lisa and I used to kick it.

"Yeah, until you kicked me out for your ignorant-ass baby mother!"

"Yo, I ain't trying to hear that shit." My mind was on one thing and one thing only—pussy.

It was times like this that I was grateful I didn't sell or rent out my old crib out Bayside area, off of Newtown Road. We pulled up to my spot, and I stumbled out the car to the front door. Once inside I fell across the couch, lit up a cigarette, and called out to Lisa, who was heading up the stairs, apparently to my bedroom.

"What you doing, girl? Get naked. You know you giving me some ass tonight."

There was no way she was staying the night at my crib and not fuck, especially since she'd fucked up my plans of getting with Diana.

"I'm going to freshen up. Meanwhile, can you pour me some wine or something to help me relax, please?" she asked while walking upstairs.

"Nah, I ain't got nothing," I replied, shaking my head.

Just then my phone rang. I noticed I had three missed calls from Jewel already. At the time, I wasn't even trying to hear nothing her ass had to say.

Minutes later Lisa had come back downstairs with one of my T-shirts on. I lifted it up, only to see her neatly shaven pussy underneath.

"Excuse you." She pulled the shirt back down then straddled me.

She tried to kiss me, but I quickly turned my head.

"What? I can't get a kiss?"

I threw her on the couch and ripped her T-shirt and underwear off.

"Why you got to be so rough?" She rolled her eyes at me.

"Shut the fuck up!"

My phone rang another four times back to back. I knew it was Jewel blowing me up.

"Touch, you just tore my bra. This is a La Perla bra and panty set. Do you know how much this cost?"

"Of course, I do. Wasn't I the one buying you that shit when we were together? I probably bought this shit you got on now," I replied, cramming my dick into her dry pussy.

I figured she wasn't in the mood yet, but I was sure it wasn't anything the "king cobra" couldn't fix. And, just as I figured, a few minutes later, I was hearing those sweet moans and groans.

"Ride this dick," I ordered after turning her over to switch positions.

I had to admit, this bitch did have some good pussy. After we had finished fucking, she quickly fell asleep.

I tried to, but Jewel kept calling. Knowing her, she was probably trying to hunt my ass down. I was never the nigga to turn my phone off, because I always figured that the one time I turned it off would be the day something happened to my mom or kids and they couldn't reach me.

But Jewel was leaving a nigga with no choice. Once phone call number fifteen had come through, I was forced to turn off my phone to get some rest. *What a day!* I thought, drifting off to sleep.

Chapter 16

"Cheating Death"

Poppo

"**G**otdamn!" I yelled as I hung up the phone with my boy.

He'd just given me the news that Calico was locked up. Most niggas would look at that shit as bad luck, but in his case, it was good luck. That nigga ain't even know he was minutes away from death. That fucking arrest saved his life. The reason I couldn't come for that nigga when he was calling me was because I was setting shit up so I could do him in. I was planning to pick him up and take him to the spot and dead his ass later in the day. But this time that nigga got away.

Ring! Ring!

I was surprised to see Jewel calling. I guess she'd heard the news too. "What up, ma?" I answered right away.

"You fucking tell me. That's what the fuck I want to

know. What the fuck is up, Poppo?" Jewel yelled in the phone between tears.

I hadn't the slightest idea what the fuck she was snapping about. "Yo, yo, relax, mami. What's going on?"

"What the fuck did you say to Touch, Poppo? He came home talking some shit about me and you in cahoots together, and I can't be trusted. He even tried to say we were fucking! That's crazy, especially since I haven't talked to you in forever. I assumed you were playing games when you stood me up, and now I hear this shit?"

Right then I knew exactly what Jewel was talking about. It looked like Touch had finally broke the news to her. I personally wondered what the fuck took that nigga so long. I expected to get this call days ago. Already prepared for the wrath, I slipped right into character, becoming Mr. Concerned and Apologetic.

"Listen, Jewel. I'm sorry, baby. I didn't mean for shit to go down that way. That was my bad. A nigga wasn't thinking."

"Did you tell him that we were fucking, Poppo?"

"Nah, I would never do that. I'm a man of my word. You got to trust me. Besides, are we fucking?" I laughed.

"Hell, no!" she snapped back.

"All right, then. Bitch-ass niggas tell a whole bunch of people stupid shit like that. I'm a real nigga. Soon, my actions will show you that. I understand if you're sitting on the sideline as a skeptic right now though, especially since the last time we were supposed to meet I never made it. But about that day, I swear, ma . . . that shit was out of my control. I was on my way and I ended up getting locked up over some bullshit."

"Things are real bad for me, Poppo," Jewel cried out. "I'm fucked up in the game right now. I don't know what to think or who to trust. You don't understand the shit I've been through. I mean, look at this shit. Me and Calico use to be together. He was my man, Poppo, and now we're fucking enemies. Sasha was my best friend, and she stabbed me in the back. Touch was all I had, and now that shit is fucked. What the fuck am I supposed to do or think?"

"I feel you, baby girl. I understand you to the fullest. But I'm saying, I'm setting shit up, ma. Please, I just need you to be a little more patient with a nigga. This shit takes time. You feel me?"

"Yeah, but I can only be patient for so long," she whimpered.

"Don't worry. I got chu. Can I bring you lunch, dinner, or anything else that would cheer you up?" I asked in a concerned tone of voice, trying to throw in a little game. I thought it was the perfect opportunity. Bitches always slipped up when they're vulnerable.

"No, thanks. I'll be all right. I'm just ready to get things going."

"I know. I am too, so let me do my thing. You screaming in my ear ain't helping either one of us."

"Okay," Jewel said before hanging up the phone.

I was relieved that I was able to calm things down and smooth shit over.

Chapter 17

"Thin Line between Love and Hate"

Sasha

I was at my parents crib in Columbia when I got the word. I kept repeating the words of Detective Tarver in my head, *"We finally got him!"* That was the greatest news I could have ever heard.

Now that I knew Calico was locked up, I could finally move freely. I still wasn't trying to testify against him, but I'd told the detectives any information I could find out about Jewel and her affiliation with TMF. I figured this was my only opportunity to finally get Jewel out the picture for good. And once she was gone, I would move in on her throne, steal her king, and rule her empire. Finally, I would be the queen that I was destined to be.

I'd planned to only give them information that pointed toward Jewel. Hell, as far as I knew, she was the mastermind behind her and Touch's little fortune anyway. She was the one with the TMF connect. Because TMF was one of the biggest organized drug rings in the United States, I knew that saying those words to the detective would be like music to his ears.

I was still on some get-money shit. I had gained so much trust from Diablo, I'd gone from delivering packages to receiving them at my address for him. I was number one on the team. He trusted me more than he did some of his close boys, which worked in my favor. The more jobs I got, the more money I made.

I had an incoming call from Diablo.

"Hello?"

"Yo, when my daughter gets dropped off at your crib, I need you to take her to VA? Can you do that for me?" Diablo spoke in code. He wanted me to take the package I received at my house to Virginia.

I excitedly agreed. "No problem."

"Cool. Come see me when she arrives."

The timing couldn't have been better. An all-expenses-paid trip to VA was exactly what the doctor ordered. This gave me the opportunity to get at Touch.

I packed my bags as I waited for the package to arrive. By the time I was finished packing, I'd received the delivery. I wasted no time packing it up and getting on the road. I ran by the club and hollered at Diablo then hit the interstate.

In eight hours flat I was in VA. I grabbed some food and got checked into my hotel and relaxed a little. I thought about calling Touch, but I wasn't sure how I could go about it. I mean, I did bust his girl in the head with a champagne bottle. I hoped he could look past that and focus more on that one night of perfect love-making we had shared.

It took a moment, but I finally got up enough courage to scroll through my phone to give him a call.

"Hello," Touch answered the phone in a fake female voice.

"Touch, stop disguising your voice."

He continued in his fake voice. "Hello. Who is this?"

"It's Sasha, fool."

"What the fuck you want?"

"Damn! It's like that? Why so much aggression?"

"What the fuck you want, Sasha?"

"Well, I'm in the area, and I was wondering if I could come check you. But before you answer, I need you to think about the last time you were in this phat pussy." I paused a minute. "Okay, now that you've had time to think about it, what's up?"

"Bitch, I'm in some phat pussy right now. And I wouldn't fuck your conniving ass with an AIDS-infected dick. Lose my number, bitch!" Touch followed his statement with a click in my ear.

That was the final straw. Touch had dissed me for the last fucking time. I didn't take rejection well. He was definitely going to feel my wrath. If he didn't know, he was about to learn that payback's a bitch. His name had officially been added to the get-back list. I was about to make his life a living hell and benefit from it all at the same time.

I called up Diablo.

"What up?"

"Oh my God, Diablo," I said, forcing out the words between fake cries.

"What's wrong?" Diablo yelled in a panic.

I purposely didn't answer. I just continued to cry uncontrollably, to add more drama to my act.

"Sasha!" Diablo yelled. "What the fuck is going on?"

"Touch robbed me," I lied. "He beat me up and robbed me."

"What the fuck you doing with that nigga?"

"I invited him over to my room to kick it. Once he got here and realized I had the package here, he straight robbed me."

"What? This nigga can't know that's my shit. Ain't no way he would fuck with my shit like that. Let me give that nigga a call."

"I'll call him on three-way. He probably won't answer your call, since he don't know the number."

I dialed Touch's phone.

Touch yelled into the phone as soon as he picked up, "Bitch, didn't I say lose my number?"

"Yo, nigga, this Diablo."

"Diablo? What the fuck you doing with that broad? What type of games y'all playing?" Touch asked, confused.

"Nah. The question is, what type of games you playing? What the fuck you doing with my shit?"

"Fuck you talking 'bout, man?"

"Sasha told me you robbed her. That's my shit, Touch."

"Man, you believe that lying-ass bitch if you want to. Fuck her! And as a matter of fact, fuck you too for calling me with that bullshit. I'm rich, nigga. I don't need your little-ass shit." Touch disconnected the call.

"Don't worry about shit," Diablo said to me. "I'll handle this shit with him. You all right though?"

"I'm banged up a little, but I'll be okay."

I was happy as hell that Diablo had played right into my little plan. I must say, Touch was right about one thing—I was very conniving and believable.

"Cool. Call me if you need anything."

Chapter 18

"A New Woman"

Jewel

"*You have reached the voicemail box of—*"
I hung up before the recording could finish. Not hearing Touch's voice and wondering what the fuck he was doing and where the hell he was at was driving me crazy. It had been an entire day since our argument, and I hadn't heard from him. I had called his phone non-stop for a whole hour straight, and all I got was straight voicemail. It had gotten to the point that I was starting to worry. I even called his mother, and she hadn't heard from him.

I didn't know what to think. I wondered if he was with another bitch. It was insulting to me, to keep being sent directly to his voicemail. I was starting to feel as if he didn't give a fuck about me or my feelings. *Was he just ignoring me because of the argument, or had he run into one of Calico's boys and was hurt or, even worse, dead?* My brain was racing.

I'd spent the past day sitting in the house, depressed and crying. I hadn't eaten anything or even bothered to wash my ass or brush my teeth. I picked up the phone to call Misty because she'd called several times earlier in the day and I didn't even bother to answer. I just wasn't in the mood for conversation.

"Hey, girl," I said, trying to sound a little upbeat.

"Jewel?" Misty asked, not even recognizing my voice.

"Yeah, it's me. What's up?"

"What's wrong, momma?"

"Girl, I'm down in the dumps. Sad as hell."

"Awwww. What's wrong, boo?" Misty asked, sounding concerned.

I explained to her the drama I had with Touch from beginning to end.

"I'm sorry to hear that. I'm coming over. Get up and get yourself together. We're gonna go out and have some dinner and drinks. Then we're gonna strategize on how to get your boo back."

"Okay. I'm getting up now. Give me about an hour."

"Cool. See you then."

I got off the phone with Misty then drug myself out of bed. I ran myself a hot bath, turned on Keyshia Cole's CD, *A Different Me,* and turned on the jets in the tub and soaked.

Thirty minutes later I was clean as a whistle and actually felt a little revived. I threw on some clothes, pulled my hair into a messy ponytail, and straightened up the house a little bit as I waited for Misty.

Ding-dong!

Misty had arrived right on time. She gave me a hug as soon as I opened the door. "Hey, hon. You ready?"

I wanted to just cry in her arms, but I took a deep breath, sucked it up, and put on a smile. "Yeah, I'm ready."

Misty tried to share words of inspiration as we headed to her truck. "This isn't a pity party," she said. "We're preparing for a victory. You're gonna get your boo back."

We ended up at a bar not far from my house called Pandemonium, which was the perfect atmosphere. We walked in and headed straight to the bar. Misty ordered our drinks as I got comfortable. Still a little shook from the New Year's incident, I skimmed the restaurant, just to get a feel of my surroundings.

"Oh my God!"

"What is it?" Misty asked, startled.

I stood up from my barstool and walked away immediately, totally ignoring her. It was like I was in a zone and no one or anything around existed as I headed toward the table in front of me.

"Well, I'm glad to know you're okay," I said in my most sarcastic tone, my heart racing. This moment, and what I would do and say, had crossed my mind many times, but now that I was faced with it, I didn't know if I was ready for it.

Touch didn't respond. He just looked up at me, disgust on his face.

"Hello? I'm talking to you. I was worried sick calling all over the place for you. I even called your mother."

"I ain't have shit to say to you," Touch said, looking down at his plate.

"You didn't have shit to say? I texted your ass nearly twenty times today. The least you could have done was let me know you were okay. Is that too much to fucking ask for, Touch?"

"I ain't have shit to say to you then, and I still don't have shit to say to you right now."

"What?" I wondered if this nigga had lost his fucking mind. Feeling disrespected, I began to get loud. "What you mean, you ain't got shit to say to me, Touch? After all the shit we've been through, you really don't have shit to say to me?"

The chick that sat beside Touch finally chimed in full of attitude. "Excuse me," she said. "I don't know if you noticed, but we're trying to have dinner here."

"Excuse me? No, excuse *you*," I responded, totally thrown off by this chick's comment. "I noticed, but I just don't give a fuck. Who the fuck are you anyway? I don't know if you noticed, but I'm wearing a ring. I'm trying to have a conversation with my fiancé. Let me repeat that—*fiancé*," I spat back, feeling like I was about to explode.

"Fiancé? Well, he wasn't your fiancé when he was all up in me last night." The chick then directed her attention toward Touch. "I see nothing has changed with you, Touch."

Dazed, I stood motionless as the bitch's words registered in my head. This whole ordeal was hitting me like a fucking freight train, head-on and with no time to run for cover. I had to wonder how we went from getting married one day to my man fucking another chick the next day. The realization sank in that my world was crumbling before my eyes.

It wasn't until I heard the chick say, "Fuck this! I'm out," that I snapped back to the moment.

"Yeah, bitch, that's the best thing for you. Be out."

The chick stopped dead in her tracks, turned around, and staring me in the face. "Or what?"

She was so close, I could feel the heat from her breath. For a moment I thought about getting out the pepper spray I carried in my handbag, but before I could do anything, I felt someone come between the chick and me.

"Or this!" Misty tossed her drink all up in the chick's face.

"We'll cross paths again," the skinny, shapeless chick with weave to her ass said, knowing she was no match for Misty and me.

I wondered how we hadn't crossed paths before. I knew Touch had a steady girlfriend before me, but the only girl I'd actually seen from his past was his baby mother. If I had to guess, this bitch probably was his ex.

"What was that about?" Misty asked.

"Nothing at all. The bitch just got a little heated because I told her to step."

"Oh, okay. I was watching from the bar the entire time. Everything looked cool, so I didn't intervene, but when I saw that bitch come in your face, I rushed over. I would have given her a beatdown if necessary."

We both laughed.

I directed my attention back toward Touch, who was pulling out money from his wallet to pay for his meal.

"Oh, so you just gonna leave, Touch? We not gonna talk about this? You don't feel like you owe me an explanation or nothing?"

"I don't owe you shit. I just want to be by myself right now. I need some space. I'll be coming over to the house to get my things." Touch dropped a hundred dollars on the table then walked away, leaving me hanging.

Chapter 19

"Doing Hard Time"

Calico

I opened my eyes and looked around at the bricks and bars surrounding me. "I can't believe this shit."

I was hoping this whole shit was a nightmare, but come to find out, I wasn't dreaming at all. My dick ached, my stomach was growling, and I needed a fucking spliff. I hopped off my bunk and headed to the phone. I hit up one of my jump-off bitches from Norfolk.

She accepted the collect call right away. "What's up, baby?"

"Fucked up, shortie. Thanks for taking the call. You know I got you."

"You know I got your back, boo."

"Look, I need you to make a call for me on three-way."

"Not a problem."

I then called out Poppo's number to her.

Poppo answered right away, "Yo."

"What up, nigga?"

"Calico. What the fuck is good, man? I heard you got snatched, nigga."

"Man, it's a long story. I'll fill you in on that shit later. Right now I need you to call my people back home and let them know what's up, so they can get shit lined up to get me out this bitch. Then I need you to handle things with your boy in A-town for me. You gonna have to hold down the fort until I get this shit straight. You feel me?"

"Nuff said, nigga. Say no more. You know I got you. I'ma jump on shit right now. Gone." Poppo hung up the phone.

A few minutes later, the recording came on, warning us we had one minute left on the phone, so we wrapped things up and ended the call.

I returned to my bunk and tried to map something out. I knew I needed to get in touch with my moms and baby mother. They were the only ones I could really depend on to handle my money and make sure the lawyer was paid.

I'd learned my lesson about letting jump-off bitches hold money. That situation I had in the past when I was fucking with Jewel had taught me well. I had got locked up and had her collect my money. When it came time for her to pay my lawyer, no money was to be found. I had to straight threaten the bitch to get my shit back.

But, to be honest, this time it was that nigga Poppo I was a little worried about. I swear, lately that nigga had been on some bullshit. I couldn't quite put my finger on it, but it was just something about him that I just wasn't feeling.

After a few days had passed, I went for my first bond hearing, and was denied. I kinda expected that shit though. These muthafuckers wasn't trying to let a nigga out. Hell, I was a major fucking flight risk. My primary residence was "across the fucking U.S." Plus, I had a number of aliases. There was no way these niggas was gonna take a chance with me.

Even with all those odds against me, Natalia, my lawyer, was still talking some good shit. She was confident that I would eventually get a bond, and was telling me it may take more than a couple of tries. One thing about her though, her word was bond. She didn't sell a nigga dreams. She was always on her shit, and never let a nigga down.

It was visiting day, and cats were getting fresh cuts and edge-ups and shit, trying to look fresh for their chicks. I wasn't fucking with none of that shit though. For one, I couldn't see myself sitting between another nigga's legs while he braided my fucking hair. Next thing I know, I ain't getting no fucking visit.

I hopped on my bunk, grabbed my dick and rubbed on it until I fell asleep.

"Burroughs!" the CO called out my last name, waking me.

"Yo!" I yelled back.

"Visit."

Damn! Who the fuck is that? I wondered who the hell had come down to check a nigga. I hadn't even bothered telling no one my visiting day.

I followed the CO to the visiting room. I was surprised to see my mother and baby mother, Corrin, when I walked out. I wondered what the fuck they were doing there and how the hell they knew my visiting day. A nigga was actually glad to see a familiar face. I was grinning from ear to ear as I sat on the steel stool across from them.

"What y'all doing here?"

"What you mean? There is no way I was gonna leave my baby alone in jail all the way across the country."

"Ma, y'all ain't have to come out here."

"Well, we wanted to make sure everything was squared away," Corrin chimed in. "We going to see Natalia and straighten her out tomorrow."

"Yeah, go 'head and pay her. That's the most important thing. Everything else can wait. You talked to Poppo?"

"Nope. That's one reason I wanted to come here. I don't know what's up with your boy. Baby, I know you ain't gonna wanna hear this, but that nigga made a pass at me."

"What the fuck you say? Corrin, don't fuck with me." I felt immediate anger come over me.

"When he came to the house to collect the things to send down South, he kept making little comments about how my ass was so phat and what he'll do to me. And some shit about you ain't gon' be around to satisfy me, so I may as well give it up to him. He was talking so crazy, I had to ask this nigga if he was drunk or on that shit. Then the next thing I know, he grabs my ass. I was sure he'd lost his fucking mind. I had to smack some sense back into his ass.

"After that I gave him the things and rushed him out of the house. I haven't heard from him since. I even called him a couple of times and left messages about the paper, but he ain't called back. He acting like he dodging niggas or something. Then I hear niggas on the streets saying Poppo talking like you ain't never getting out, and he's the new boss. This nigga can't be trusted, baby."

"What?" It was almost like I could literally feel my blood boiling inside as I listened to the words Corrin spoke.

It felt as though my back was up against the wall. I was ready to kill a nigga, but I knew beating another nigga's ass in jail to blow off steam wasn't going to do nothing but add more charges to my rap sheet. One of the worst feelings in the world was knowing a bitch-ass nigga was tripping on the streets and it ain't shit you can do about it.

After my visit with my moms and baby mother, I wondered how the fuck I was going to make it through.

Five days had passed, which felt more like months, and the two special ladies in my life had already paid my lawyer in full. As usual, she was on her grind. I knew the time would soon arrive when I would be released from

Virginia Beach hell, AKA Virginia Beach jail. And I knew when I was released I'd be on an unstoppable mission to get my fucking money. The first stop on the road would be a visit to check Poppo. I wondered if he was going to like having a gun in his damn mouth, or a knife clinging to his throat.

Chapter 20

"New Man in Town"

Poppo

"What up, Poppo?" Raz gave me a pound as I walked in the barbershop.

"Ain't shit, nigga. 'Look like money, smell like money,' you know the song, nigga," I said, feeling on top of the world.

Now that Calico was locked up, I was the king of the castle. I'd used the product I'd gotten from his baby mother and flipped it a few times. Finally a nigga was making his own money and not taking orders. This was the opportunity I'd been waiting for. From the looks of things Calico was never gonna see daylight, so I was on some real "fuck-you" shit. I had his shit, I was doing what the fuck I wanted to, and I wasn't afraid to let niggas know it. I had a new attitude. It was time for niggas on the street to know Poppo wasn't Calico's little bitch.

I walked through the barbershop straight to the back,

where some dudes were playing a dice game. Feeling a little lucky with my new profile, I got in on the game.

Deebo, one of the guys in the dice game, held the dice in front of a chick who was watching the game. "Blow on these dice for me, baby." She blew on the dice. Then he rolled them. "Bam! Seven! Pay up, nigga, pay up!" Deebo hit, and I lost one hundred dollars just like that.

"Damn, baby girl! You must be good luck. Let me rub these dice on that ass this time. Nah, matter of fact, let me rub them on your ass, pussy, and titties."

"Man, shut the fuck up and roll the fucking dice!" I yelled, getting pissed off by the bullshit this nigga was doing.

"Man, fuck you, Poppo!" he snapped back.

Deebo wasn't no big nigga on the streets, but he was known for bullying a nigga and taking their shit. Just like his namesake from the movie *Friday*, Deebo was the neighborhood bully.

"Fuck you say, nigga?" I stood up. If Deebo had the chance to tackle me, it would be "game over."

Deebo stood up now, towering over me. "Nigga, you heard me!"

"Nigga, you better recognize what the fuck is good and step the fuck back. I run these fucking streets, nigga." I had to man up. If I gave the slightest indication of weakness, this bully would have definitely tried to overpower me.

"Whatever, duke. You come in this bitch talking shit like you on top of the fucking world when just the other week you was in here crying like a fucking baby talking about how Calico don't respect your bitch ass. Nigga, shut the fuck up!" Deebo took two fingers and mushed me in my forehead.

When Deebo stood up and mushed me in my head, he had taken shit to the next level. I knew it was either do or die at that point. So, with my reputation on the line, I knew I couldn't back down. I pulled out my gun and gave him one big forceful strike across the face.

Bam!

One hit and the dude fell to the ground.

"Now who's the bitch?" I said to him as blood flowed from his lip.

"Daaaammmmmmnnnn! You just got knocked the fuck out!" Another guy jokingly quoted the words from the movie *Friday* when Deebo got knocked out.

As everyone else busted out in laughter at his antics, I walked away.

The constant joking must have been too much for him to handle because, just as I got to the door of the barbershop, I heard a lot of commotion behind me. Before I could turn around, I heard shots.

Pop! Pop! Pop!

I dove between two cars and pulled my gun out. I looked up to see dude rushing to a car. I shot back at him. *Bam! Bam!*

I watched as he fell to the ground. I wasn't sure where he was hit, but at least he was down. I jumped in my whip and peeled off, never looking back.

* * *

Ring! Ring! Not even a whole hour after I'd left the barbershop, I got a call from one of the barbers.

"What up, Mike?"

"It ain't good, nigga. You know old boy ain't make it. The cop was up here and everything, nigga. Ain't nobody but niggas is out to get you, duke. Deebo boys say, as soon as they see you, it's straight gunplay, no talk."

"What you talking about, Mike?" I played stupid, not knowing if the cops were around or if this nigga was trying to set me up.

"I'm just letting you know the deal. Watch your back, homeboy. Watch your back." Mike then hung up.

I really ain't give a fuck if dude lived or not. As long as I was still breathing, that's all that mattered. Fuck him and his weak-ass crew. I'd been bitched out for the last time and wasn't backing down from no nigga, so any cat who wanted could bring it.

And, as a matter of fact, fuck Mike too for calling me with that shit. There was no way he was gonna get me to talk about that shit on the phone. Like I told that nigga, I didn't know what the fuck he was talking about. Right at that point, permanent amnesia had set in. I had no recollection of those events. Who's Deebo? And what barbershop?

Chapter 21

"Get Your Boo"

Jewel

An entire week had passed, and I hadn't seen or heard from Touch. He didn't even come to the house to collect his things. I felt so depressed and hurt. I'd spend days in bed. I didn't even bother to bathe or put on clothes. I barely ate anything, and I'd completely stopped taking my birth control. I figured, *What's the use?* There was no longer a man in my life anyway.

I would've never guessed in a million years that Touch and I would've ended like this. Part of me wanted to fight for my man, but another part of me hated him. I couldn't understand how he could move on to the next chick so quickly. No matter now much shit we went through, being with another man had never crossed my mind.

I began to think about this new chick sitting on my throne. *If another chick came in, where would that leave me? What about this empire that Touch and I had built?*

The reality of things was really beginning to settle in. The fact of the matter was, without Touch my entire life would change. Sure, I had the connection with TMF and could get my hands on all kinds of coke, but it was Touch who knew how to push that shit and bring the money in, and who invested in real estate and made our money legit.

Truthfully, I knew nothing about the business and wouldn't be able to survive without him. One thing I did know for sure, there was no way I could go from the top to rock bottom—all at the hands of another bitch. The more I thought about things, the more panic began to set in.

Desperately needing someone to talk to, I called up Misty. She was the only person I had in my corner.

Misty answered the phone in her usual perky voice, "What's up, girly?"

"Touch still hasn't come home, Misty. I haven't even spoken to him since that night at the restaurant. I don't know what to think or do. I really think it's over between us," I said, bursting into tears.

"Oh, you poor baby. I'm so sorry. Do you want me to come over?" Misty was so comforting.

"No, Misty. I don't want to keep dragging you into my affairs. I shouldn't have even called you."

"Jewel, I'm here for you. That's what friends are for. Talk to me, honey. For some reason, I feel like there is more to your pain. What's the matter, Jewel? Are you pregnant?"

Between tears, I sobbed. "No, I'm not pregnant."

"Well, then what is it?"

"It's just that . . ." I paused, pulling myself together enough to slow up the tears.

I wasn't sure how to explain my dilemma, but Misty was being so kind, so understanding. Maybe because I hadn't been close to any other woman since Sasha, the next thing I knew, I had blurted out my whole life story. I told her all about me and Touch from beginning to end. I told her how we started off as friends and how we built our empire. I explained to her how Calico and Touch used to be partners in the game and how Calico and I hooked up. I even told her about how Sasha was my friend turned lover and how she turned on me.

"Anyway, I'm afraid without Touch I will have nothing. My life will completely fall apart, and I will lose everything I've worked so hard for." I started wailing with a whole new fresh set of tears.

Meantime, Misty didn't say a word. I didn't know if she was shocked by my story, or what the deal was. Then finally I heard a sniffle that broke the silence.

"Misty, are you crying?"

"I'm sorry. I'm supposed to be supporting you. It's just that you're so much like me. Everything you're going through, I've experienced. I feel your pain, baby. Matter of fact, I'm on my way over." Misty hung up the phone before I could protest.

In thirty minutes flat Misty had arrived. I looked a mess as I opened the door. I hadn't had the energy to do anything to myself. My normally long, thick, curly hair sat in a tangled mess on top of my head.

"Hey, boo." Misty hugged me as soon as I opened the door.

"Hey, girl," I responded in my most depressed tone.

"Wow! You really look stressed," Misty said, noticing my ragged look. "I know what you need right now."

"I need Touch here with me right now telling me we're still going to do the damn thing and get married. He acts like he don't even give a fuck about me. How can he treat me this way? It hurts to the core."

Misty stroked my tangled hair. "Everything will be all right."

I called those five words "the girlfriend's anthem." A true girlfriend sure could tell you that everything would work out, no matter how bleak shit looked. I was grateful that Misty had moved up from acquaintance level to being one of my girls.

"No, it won't," I said, seeing no light at the end of this dark, dark tunnel.

"Yes, it will. We're gonna get your man back," Misty said. "Now, this is what you're going to do."

"What?" I said between sniffles.

"You're going to stop by Victoria's Secret and buy the sexiest negligee you can find. You're going to cook his favorite meal and plan to have a romantic candle light dinner."

"But I haven't heard from him in a week. How can I get him home?"

"You call him and tell him you want to talk. When he shows up, you let him be the man, and think everything is his idea, but then you screw his brains out."

"Oh God. It hurts so bad. I hope this works," I said, feeling hopeless.

"Hon, I know it hurts. I've been there too a few times myself. There aren't too many men who can say they've had my heart. I know you want Touch back in your arms; it's what we both want. But right now, I'm going to get you a cup of herbal tea, so you can relax a little. I brought some over from my place. Give me five minutes, and I'll be right back."

Misty headed toward the kitchen and came back five minutes later with a cup of steaming hot tea.

I took a sip. "Misty, this tea is good." It soothed my scratchy throat.

"I figured you would like it. I drink it when I'm stressed. Next, let's get you cleaned up," she ordered, heading into the bathroom to run bath water for me.

After a few minutes, my bath was ready, and Misty ordered me into the bathroom.

It was like a load had been lifted off my back as I soaked in the tub with the jets blowing. While Misty washed and combed through my hair ever so gently, I closed my eyes, trying to relax. Although it was sort of awkward at first, once I relaxed, it felt good. Misty washed my hair and bathed me as though I was her patient and she was my nurse.

Since I'd been taking care of Touch for a while, it felt

good for someone to finally take care of me for a damn change. All washed up and totally relaxed, I climbed out of the tub.

After directing me to lay face down on the bed, Misty didn't hesitate massaging my body with Oil of Olay lotion. Suddenly finding myself in another awkward moment, my body immediately tensed up.

"Relax, Jewel," Misty said. "Everything I'm doing for you, you should do for your man. Consider this a lesson and take notes."

I took a deep breath and slowly exhaled, trying to relax. I closed my eyes and indulged in the moment. I must say, once I was relaxed, I was able to realize Misty was a damn good massage therapist. Her caress was slow, deep, and an enjoyable pain.

"How does this feel?" she whispered in my ear.

I could feel the heat from her breath on my neck. It sent a sexual sensation down my spine. "Mmmm! Better than any massage I've ever had."

"Good. It only gets better." Misty started caressing my neck with kisses and then licking my ears with her tongue. She turned me over to face her.

I knew exactly where this was headed. Part of me couldn't believe what was happening, but then another part of me wanted so badly to continue.

I gave in to my sexual urge, and we began kissing. While our tongues met, Misty took two fingers of her right hand and starting massing my clit. For a split second, my mind couldn't help but to drift to Sasha. She'd once touched me in this same way, and we'd shared similar sexual experiences.

Once our tongues drifted apart, Misty's tongue found its way to my left breast. She went back and forth sucking on my nipple and gently biting it. By now my pussy was dripping wet.

Misty started licking my clit, and before I knew it, I came in her mouth.

"Misty, what the fuck just happened?" I said between breaths. I'd cum so hard, I was nearly out of breath.

"Ssshhh! Don't worry, baby," Misty said gently.

I obeyed and didn't say anything more. I wasn't sure where things were headed next, and honestly, I wasn't too concerned. For the first time in days, I was totally relaxed, and I'd just released a load of tension.

As my worries drifted away, I dozed off to sleep.

Exhausted from all the events of the past days and busting a huge nut the previous night, I didn't wake until the next day.

I woke to the smell of bacon and eggs. I walked in the kitchen to see Misty cooking up a grand breakfast that included blueberry waffles and omelets. With Touch on my mind, a fresh burst of energy, and Misty by my side, I decided to do just as Misty had advised the night before and called Touch.

"Yeah," Touch greeted me on the phone after I dialed his number.

I was nervous as hell. I didn't want to take no for an

answer of him seeing me. But Misty was right by my side, coaching me along.

"Hey, baby," I said.

He sighed. "What you want, Jewel?"

"Well, um, I was wondering if you could come over to the house for a bit. I just want to talk," I suggested, keeping my fingers crossed.

"I'll be over in a few hours. I need to get a few things anyway," he responded and hung up the phone in my ear.

I didn't even care that he'd hung up on me. I was just happy he'd agreed to come over.

Three hours gave Misty and me plenty of time to go to the mall to Victoria's Secret and to the grocery store to get two fresh T-bone steaks and a few sweet potatoes to bake. I planned to smother them in apple butter, cinnamon, and nutmeg, just the way Touch liked it. Next, I planned to cut up a tossed salad topped with French dressing and croutons. For dessert, it was going to be apple crumb cobbler.

Walking around in my black lace teddy and five-inch stiletto heels gave me confidence. I felt sexy, like every man on earth wanted a piece of my pussy. I began to rehearse in my mind what I would say to Touch, remembering to watch my tone. The last thing I wanted to do was get him mad and then have him storm off on me like the last time.

Chapter 22

"When a Man's Fed Up"

Touch

Jewel greeted me at the door, "Hey, boo." She tried to kiss me on the lips, but I turned, and she caught my cheek instead.

While walking in the house, I was on my cell phone patching up things with Lisa. I didn't know what Jewel had in mind, but this one night wasn't gonna change how I felt about things between us.

I went into the kitchen to grab a Heineken from the fridge then glanced over at the food that Jewel cooked. *Damn! My favorite*, I thought as my mouth began to water, but I refused to voice it. Instead, I acted like it didn't even faze me.

I noticed Jewel let out a big sigh, I guess, to refrain from getting pissed and going the fuck off on me.

I grinned to myself and continued my phone conversation. "Yeah," I replied, walking over to the living room to sit down on the couch.

"Baby, how was your day?" Jewel inquired.

"A'ight," I responded.

"Well, maybe I can make it end on a wonderful note." Jewel began to massage my shoulders.

She poured vanilla-scented oil in to her hands, rubbed them together to get the oil nice and warm then caressed my shoulders deeply. I couldn't deny, that shit felt damn good too.

"How's that?" Jewel asked, after giving me a five-star full body massage.

"That was on point," I said, finally relaxed enough to notice how enticing her nightie was.

My dick began to rise as I watched Jewel's ass bounce in her thong as she walked over to the bar to make me a Grey Goose on the rocks. I turned on the television and flipped through the channels as I gulped down the drink she'd made me.

"Uuummm . . . is this for me?" she asked, rubbing my now fully erect dick.

I didn't respond. I just gave her a grin and swallowed the rest of the liquor I had in the glass.

Noticing my glass was empty, Jewel immediately grabbed it and headed back to the bar to make me round two. This time before returning she turned on R. Kelly's *and* Jay-Z's *The Best of Both Worlds* CD, lit some candles, and dimmed the lights. Upon returning to the couch, she took the remote from my hand and turned off the television.

As I sipped on my second glass of Grey Goose, Jewel slipped off my pants. She grabbed my dick and started to lick the tip of my head, gently getting it nice and moist. Then she moved down the shaft, licking it up and down a couple of times then continuing to my balls. A tingling sensation filled my body as she engulfed my balls in her mouth one at a time.

By this time my dick was so hard, it felt at though it was gonna explode. Just when I thought I couldn't take anymore, Jewel gripped my dick and began deep-throating it just the way I liked it. I spread my legs, grabbed a handful of her hair, and pushed her face deep in my lap. I closed my eyes and let my head fall back as I absorbed each second of this goodness. One thing for sure, there was no denying that Jewel gave a hell of a blowjob.

"You like that?"

"Suck that shit, bitch!" I grabbed Jewel's hair even tighter, forcing her head down farther onto my rock-hard dick.

"Aaahhh fuck!" Jewel started to gag as my cum rushed out the tip of my dickhead and hit the back of her throat. She sucked off every drip and swallowed like she was eating her favorite ice cream.

That shit was just foreplay for me. I grabbed Jewel and ripped her lingerie off. I pinned her to the carpeted floor and forced three of my fingers into her soaking wet pussy.

"You giving my pussy to another nigga?"

"No, baby. You know this is yours."

"Maybe you giving the ass up." I forced my thumb in her ass.

She screamed out in pain. "Aaaaahhhh! No, baby. No, I'm not!"

Instead of sucking on her nipple, I bit it. There was no fucking lovemaking this night. To make love, a nigga had to be in love, and honestly I felt no love for her at the time. The thought of her betraying me killed all feelings of love I had for her.

"Ah shit!" Jewel cried out. "Touch, you're killing me, baby."

I pushed in even deeper and harder as I began to reach my peak. "Take the dick, Jewel."

"Baby, please pull out. Don't cum in me, Touch."

"Where you want it? You gonna take it on your titties or on your ass?"

"Wherever you want, baby. Just pull it out."

"Aaaaahhhhh!" After I banged the pussy up DMX-style as in the movie *Belly*, I came deep inside her, totally ignoring her request to pull out.

"Touch, you came in me?" she asked, feeling my wetness drip from inside her.

"Yep," I said as I jumped up.

I quickly headed upstairs. I wasn't trying to hear that shit Jewel was talking. If it was my pussy like she had just claimed minutes earlier, then I was free to do whatever I like with it.

I jumped in the shower and freshened up then headed to the bedroom and grabbed some clothes. I made sure I packed enough things to last me for a while. I didn't want to make another trip back over to the house anytime soon.

"Where are you going?" Jewel asked.

I guess me packing and leaving wasn't in keeping with her plans. "Back to my crib," I told her. "I'm out."

"We haven't talked yet."

"Like I said, I'm out," I repeated, and turned to leave.

Jewel ran into the kitchen and grabbed the two plates of food that she had prepared while I was in the shower. "Don't forget your dinner!" She threw the two plates of food up against the wall near where I was standing.

I didn't give a fuck, as long as she didn't throw that shit at me. I heard her on the phone as I continued to gather my last few items.

"Hello, Misty," she said between sobs. "He's leaving."

Not wanting to be a part of the drama, I rushed out the door, slamming it behind me.

I didn't even get out of the neighborhood before my phone started to ring. Assuming it was Jewel, I didn't even bother to answer.

The phone rang another three times. After the third time, I noticed it was a different number, so I answered. "Yeah."

"Hey, Touch. This is Misty, Jewel's friend," the voice said from the other end of the phone.

"Okay. So what the fuck you want, Misty?" I never really got a good vibe from her.

"Touch, we really need to talk. Jewel is talking crazy. I think she's gonna have a nervous breakdown or do something crazy. You both may be in danger. If you have a few minutes, can you meet me at Silverfish? It's a bar down at the oceanfront, on Seventeenth Street."

"I know where it is. Give me about an hour," I said then hung up the phone.

I really wasn't interested in how the fuck Jewel felt, but when Misty said she was talking crazy and we both may be in danger, that shit caught my attention. I was hoping Jewel wasn't crazy enough to try to call the police on a nigga. I didn't play those types of games. I'd had more than one run-in with shit like that from my stupid-ass baby mother.

One hour turned into two hours as I made a quick stop by Mo Dean's before going to the oceanfront, but I eventually made it to the bar. I was surprised to see Misty still there waiting.

"What up, Misty?"

"Hey, Touch. Thanks for meeting me. Have a seat. I'll buy you a drink."

Misty pressed IGNORE on her constantly ringing phone. The wise side of me was pretty sure that was probably Jewel blowing up her cell phone.

"What did you want to talk about?" I asked as I grabbed a seat next to her at the bar and made myself comfortable.

"Well, I wanted to talk you about Jewel. She's been crying constantly since you left. She's hysterical. She's talking like she can't go on another day without you."

Blah, blah, blah, blah. Misty's words began to go in one ear and out the other. I didn't know if it was the two double shots of Grey Goose I'd drank at Mo Dean's prior to meeting Misty or what, but my mind was definitely wandering other places.

Places like all over her body, to be exact. This bitch was sitting with her legs wide open. I had a bird's-eye view of her "camel toe" through her black tights. The sight of her fat pussy instantly made my wood stand up.

"Yo, let me get a Long Island Iced Tea for the lady," I said to the bartender, a drink that was guaranteed to get Misty a little tipsy.

"Thanks. But do you hear what I'm saying about Jewel?"

"What about Jewel?" I asked, knowing I hadn't heard anything she'd said about her.

"Touch, she loves you very much. Look, I don't know the whole story from beginning to end with the two of you, but I do know that right now she's hurting to know that you think she betrayed you, because she didn't," Misty explained.

"Hmm. Is that so?"

"Yes," she declared.

"Let's take a walk," I suggested, noticing that Misty had already finished the drink I'd ordered.

"Okay. I could use the fresh air," she agreed, obviously feeling a little tipsy.

I dropped a few dollars on the bar to cover the tab and pulled out a cigarette to light when I hit the door.

We walked all the way down to Eighth Street, where the tourists and locals were nowhere to be found. By this point the conversation had moved from Jewel to more interesting things. It felt like only the two of us, the beach, moon, and the stars just existed. This was the perfect setting for sex in my mind. For a moment I felt like Jamie Foxx, and I didn't know if I should blame it on the Henny or the Goose, but the more I looked at Misty, the sexier she was.

I kept making subtle passes and small flirtations with her. Although she resisted, I could tell, with a little more work, she would be dropping those tights and lifting her flowered shirt. We made our way back to the bar. We stopped and talked a minute outside while I finished up my cigarette.

"You know them?" Misty said, pointing to a car that drove by slowly.

Unable to see who was in the car, I watched as they drove to the end of the parking lot and turned around. There was no one else in the parking lot other than me and her, so I figured they had to be watching one of us. A part of me wondered if Jewel had hooked up with someone and decided to stalk a nigga. After all, Misty did say she was talking some crazy shit.

I took a long pull from my cigarette as I waited patiently for the car to come back around. The closer it got, the more I focused in on the people inside. It wasn't until they'd gotten up on us again that I'd realized who it was.

"Get—" I tried to warn Misty to get down, but before I could finish my sentence, shots had already rang out.

I jumped to the ground behind a car as I pulled out

my gun. From there I shot back. I looked up to see Misty right beside me firing just as many shots.

"Come with me!" Misty, who was like a miniature Rambo, grabbed my arm and pulled me toward her truck.

Moments later, we were in her truck, and the people who were shooting after us had sped off.

"What the fuck was that?" Misty asked, while speeding toward the interstate.

"I'm sorry, ma. I feel real fucked up right now. I never meant to put you in danger like that. I had no idea."

"Danger? I love danger. It's kind of sexy."

Misty had my head fucked up with her response. "Oh yeah?"

"Yep! So who was that? Was that the same dude from the club on New Year's?"

"Nah. It's a little more complicated than that. This is some beef I shouldn't even have. This broad I fucked with one time set me up. She lied to this nigga and said I beat her up, because I won't fuck with her." I told Misty the least I could about my situation with Sasha and Diablo.

"Damn! That sounds like some 'fatal attraction' shit. How long did you fuck with her?"

"For real, I didn't even fuck with her. I just fucked the bitch one night."

"Wow! You must have really put it down for her to be acting like that over a one-night stand. Umph!" Misty cut her eyes at me.

I wasn't a mind reader, but if I had to read her eyes, they were definitely saying, "I wish I could have a taste of that good dick."

"Oh yeah, the dick is good, no doubt, but it's more to it with that bitch. The bitch is just straight grimy. She'll do anything for a dollar."

"So what more is it? Like, how is she so grimy?" Misty seemed really interested in my story.

"To make a long story short, she was Jewel's best friend. I always felt like she was envious of Jewel. She wanted everything Jewel had, the clothes, shoes, jewelry, cars, houses, and even me. Sad to fucking say, but the bitch got all of it. Yeah, she stole from Jewel to get the material shit, but she wasn't suppose to get me. My stupid ass should have never fucked her."

I explained how shit went down.

"So you cheated on Jewel with her best friend?" Misty seemed shocked.

"Nah. We weren't together yet," I explained to Misty, hoping that fucking Jewel's friend wouldn't ruin my chances of fucking her.

"Mm-hmm." Misty grunted as though she didn't believe me, yet it seemed to turn her on. "You're a bad boy." She continued, "Well, I don't think it's safe for you to go back to the bar. I can just take you home if you like."

I readily agreed. "That's cool."

My mind was so fucked up as we drove, I couldn't even think straight. I couldn't believe that bitch Sasha could have gotten me fucking killed. If it wasn't for Misty peeping them out, I could have been bleeding on

guys I was supposed to deliver the package to. I
as he talked to them on the phone.

man, I got you," Diablo said. "I know shit got
p, but I ain't even trying to hold on to niggas'
ou know what I mean? I'm saying, that's why
now."

was explaining his ass off. From the looks of
iggas was really pissed off.

he got off the phone, I asked him, "Everything

man," he said with a distressed look on his

ure?"

that nigga Touch really fucking my shit up.
hell of a loss I'm taking right now, but I gotta
n niggas to keep business going, ya dig?"
you."

split second, I almost felt bad for stealing from
but I really couldn't be certain that it was actu-
that I was feeling, especially since I'd never felt
ore. The way I saw it, shit happens, so charge it
ame.

Diablo set his boys straight, he headed back to
Me, on the other hand, I had to stay back to
ay to get rid of the drugs I'd taken from him. I
he slightest idea who I could go to.

mined to get that money, I used my only re-
I headed to the strip club, The Hot Spot. As an

the concrete. Two times in a matter of a few months I'd
escaped death. I couldn't say shit. I just sat in silence.

"Okay, where to?" Misty said, interrupting my moment of silence.

I gave her directions to my crib, and minutes later, we
were pulling up in my driveway.

"Would you like to come in?" I offered.

"Sure."

Misty followed me through the door. Once inside, we
got comfortable on the couch.

"You okay, Touch?" she asked, noticing the worry on
my face.

"Just a little stressed out. This is two encounters with
death I've had in a short time. Worse, I could have gotten you killed. Basically, you're the reason I'm here.
What the fuck you doing with a gun anyway? And where
the hell did you learn to shoot like that?"

"First of all, don't worry about me. I'm used to this,
Touch. I've lived this life before. My ex-boyfriend was
heavy into the drug game too, so I was ducking and
dodging bullets and had to be on point every day."

Something about Misty's statement made me stop
and think. *What the fuck she means, "into the drug game
too"? Who the fuck said I was in the drug game?* I'd hoped
Jewel's ass didn't run her mouth to this bitch. I'd told
Jewel time and time again not to trust anyone, especially no bitch. You think she would have learned her
lesson from Sasha.

"I know it must be stressful." Misty stroked my face as
she spoke to me.

"Stressful ain't the word, ma. When I first got shot, I wondered if I would ever be back to my old self. Now I'm better, and I've got to wonder if I'd live to see the next day. I've got beef coming in every direction, and on top of that, I don't even know if I can trust the chick I was gonna make my wife. Right now I feel like it's me against the world. Real talk." For the first time, I was able to express the shit that had been on my mind.

"Aaawww, you poor baby." Misty wrapped her arms around me and playfully kissed my cheek.

Seeing this as the perfect opportunity, I began to kiss her. And, just like I figured, she didn't resist. I slid my hand underneath her loose blouse and began to massage her breast. One touch of her nipple and my manhood rose to the occasion.

"Uuummm," Misty moaned.

I gently laid her down, and she assisted me in taking her shirt off.

One by one I sucked her breasts, while slowly sliding my hand into her panties. I had to be sure to make each move right. I didn't want to take the chance of her resisting and deciding not to go through with things.

Once my hands were in her panties, I buried my fingers deep between her fat pussy lips. Feeling the thickness and moisture alone of her pussy made me want to bust. No longer able to resist, I pulled off my jeans, slipped on a jimmy hat, and before I knew it, I was all up that fat pussy I had been admiring earlier.

Chapte

"Charge It to

Sasha

*D*amn! What a fucking night
the door to my hotel roo
and I had rolled up on Touch.
Diablo to believe Touch had ro
way he could run into Touch an
wasn't expecting to be in the mi
even more shocking was seeing
bar with another chick. From w
Jewel was getting married, and fr
they were really into each other.

A part of me was actually kind
opportunity to fire shots though. M
at that bitch Touch was with. If I c
no one would. I'd rather destroy t
other bitch sit on the throne.

After our little incident, Diabl

ex-stripper, I knew a lot of the local as well as out-of-town drug dealers that hung out there.

Walking into the strip club, I didn't notice too many familiar faces. People would come and go at the strip club all the time. Stripping wasn't a line of work that exactly guaranteed job stability. One day you're there, the next day you're not. One day the money is good, the next day it's not. But even with all those downfalls, bitches still couldn't break away from the strip game. I guess it was the fast money that was so damn addictive. Just like niggas with the drug game, it was hard to let go.

"Malibu, girl, is that you?" a voice called out, addressing me by my dance name.

"It sure is," I replied back to Candy and hugged her.

Candy, her real name Jennifer, was veteran to the strip game. She was actually the person responsible for my pole skills. She taught me how to work that pole in every way imaginable.

"How you been?" she asked, looking me up and down. "You coming back to work?"

Don't you wish, bitch, I thought, knowing exactly what was going through her head.

It wasn't unusual for a current stripper to examine an ex-stripper in such a manner. I knew she was looking for any signs that I was struggling or doing bad. When a chick stops stripping, other chicks seem to think she has this I'm-better-than-you attitude. But in reality the current strippers are jealous of the ex-stripper, because they wish they were in the ex-stripper's shoes and had the same opportunity to stop dancing themselves. So if a chick happens to be one of those females that are fortunate enough to stop dancing and she comes in the strip club, the current dancer is always gonna be looking for something negative to say.

"I'm fine, girl. Just dropping through. I'm not here for work." I put any suspicion Candy had to rest then switched the subject. "How's Lamont doing?"

"Next month he'll be six."

Candy pulled out her cell phone to show me the latest picture of her son. He was a real cutie with his two front teeth missing. Looking at that picture instantly made me miss my boys.

"I'm glad I ran into you. I need a little bit of information and help."

"Whatcha need, boo? You know I got your back."

"What I need to know is, where's the ballers at? Where's the niggas that's moving major weight around here?"

"See that nigga in the corner by the pool table? He goes by the name Murdock. That's one of the heaviest niggas that be coming to the club. That's who you want to get at."

Candy assumed I was looking for a nigga to take care of me or to run some tricks with, but that was better for me. The less that bitch knew, the better.

"Thanks, girl. Do me a favor. Have the bartender send him over whatever he is drinking." I handed her a hundred-dollar bill.

I quickly went to the bathroom to look myself over and make sure my boobs were sitting up pretty and nice. Women would pay to have boobs like mine, but lucky me, I was just blessed with an awesome rack. Besides this fat cat, that was one of my greatest assets, and men couldn't keep their eyes off them.

After his drink arrived, Murdock looked around to see who sent him his bottle of Nuvo. I raised my matching glass of Nuvo to him and nodded my head, giving him a seductive smile.

After twenty minutes or so, I headed over to him.

"Hmm. I'm a little impressed. I ain't never had a female buy me a bottle, or even a drink, as a matter of fact. And you are?" He smiled at me.

I gave him a fake name and grinned back at him. "My name is Cara."

"It's nice to meet you, Cara. So what's up with you, little momma?"

"Well, I got some birds that are ready to move, and word on the streets is, you the nigga I should be hollering at," I explained with much confidence, although inside I felt a little uneasy. Normally I wouldn't take these types of chances, but I needed to get rid of Diablo's product, and fast. My back was against the wall.

"How much you want for them?"

We negotiated pricing. He got over a little, but a bitch was desperate, and anything was a profit for me, considering it wasn't my shit to begin with.

"A'ight den, it's settled. All I need to know is where and when?"

"In an hour, meet me in the parking lot of Military Circle Mall near the movie theater," I said, figuring that was a pretty safe place.

An hour came and went. I swear, muthafuckers didn't know the meaning of being on time. Murdock was running only ten minutes late, but each minute I waited felt like an eternity. I sat there nervous as hell and shaking. This should have been a smooth transaction.

I saw a couple of guys pulling up next to me in an Escalade. I put one in the head and held the gun by my side, just in case some shit popped off. The two unknown guys stood by my driver and passenger door barricading it.

What the hell is going on? Before I could process anything, one of the guys was in my face.

"Roll the window down!" he ordered.

I refused to roll the window down as he instructed.

"Do what the fuck I say and I won't blow your stupid ass up," he explained, holding up a grenade.

A grenade? This nigga can't be serious. I figured this had to be some type of joke so I yelled at him, "I ain't doing shit!"

He giggled. "Your ass will be blown to pieces."

I reached toward the gearshift to put my car in drive to pull off from this stupid-ass nigga.

"Not so fast."

Bling!

Before I could react, my window was broken, and glass was shattered all over my face.

144

"Hey, Cara, or should I say Sasha," Murdock stepped in and greeted me.

I wondered how the fuck he knew who I really was. "I'm not Sasha. My name is—"

"Yo, I'm not trying to hear shit you got to say. Hand me over that bag,"

Murdock cut me off mid-sentence.

"I am not giving you the drugs."

Bam! Murdock punched me in the side of my face with one hand and pulled me out the window of the car with the other. Then I felt the barrel of a gun pressed against my cheek.

Once my head stopped spinning and the stars before my eyes disappeared, I turned around to see a fucking AK in my face. That's when I started to realize this wasn't a joke at all. These niggas were literally ready for war, and I wasn't gonna put up a fight. I knew this would be a battle I would lose. The thought of my sons were still fresh in my head.

"Put that shit up, nigga. Y'all couldn't wait for an opportunity to pull out the toys, huh?" Murdock barked. "Y'all niggas don't need all that shit for this little bitch."

Bam! I caught another punch to the face.

"Okay, okay, I'll give you the bag."

"See . . . all it takes is a little manhandling." Murdock laughed.

I struggled to my feet and headed toward the car. I opened the front door pretending I was going for the bag but grabbed my gun instead.

Blap! Murdock's boy hit me in the face with the butt

of the gun. He'd obviously gotten a glimpse of me heading for my piece. "I told you this shit would come in handy."

By this time blood was running down my face profusely, and my eyes were nearly swollen shut. I grabbed the bag and handed it to Murdock.

"I was hoping you would choose life." Murdock snatched the bag away. He quickly hopped back in his truck and sped off.

Karma's a real bitch. I shook my head in disappointment and exhaled. "Fuck you, karma! You bitch!" I yelled out loud.

I grabbed some napkins out of the glove box and put it on my bleeding wound then put my car in drive and drove away empty-handed.

Chapter 24

"Murder for Hire"

Jewel

Severely depressed, frustrated, and tired of Touch ignoring me, I headed to Applebee's to pick up my favorite takeout order, buffalo wings with extra sauce and extra blue cheese dressing on the side, and French fries. I was hoping it would cheer me up. I'd tried calling Misty several times but couldn't reach her. I figured it would have been nice to have a girls' night out and discuss how things went when she met with Touch. But after calling her four times and texting her six times, I was probably becoming a bugaboo, which wasn't intentional. But I was really anxious to know what Touch had to say.

I have to admit, I was kind of upset when Misty didn't answer my calls, but I had to realize she had a life of her own, not to mention a very demanding job. Basically I had to check myself and appreciate all the time she'd already taken to truly listen about how I felt. Misty had provided comfort throughout my struggles with Touch. What more could a friend ask for?

The hostess greeted me with a smile as I walked through the restaurant door. "Hi. Welcome to Applebee's."

"Hello. I'm here to pick up a takeout order. The first name is Jewel," I explained, taking off my sunglasses.

"It's not ready yet. You're welcome to wait at the bar or right here by the sitting lounge," she offered. "I'll call you when it's ready."

"Thank you. I'll wait at the bar," I replied and walked over to the bar and took a seat.

"Hi. What can I get for you?" the bartender asked in the midst of taking another waiter's handwritten order.

"A pomegranate martini," I replied, hoping a nice drink would calm my nerves. After all, Applebee's pomegranate martini was my favorite.

Since me and Touch's fallout, there were times I couldn't get my hands to stop shaking. It was like my nerves had taken over me and my anxiety level was off the charts. I was still in shock that Touch had actually left me because he thought I was fucking a nothing-ass nigga like Poppo. Plus, on top of everything, he had the audacity to be fucking another bitch, as if that was okay. The thought of this whole situation made my temples tighten. I could feel a tension headache coming on. I was even more pissed that I went through all the trouble to mend things between us, and he comes over and fucks me and leaves, like I was some chick off the streets. I couldn't even get him to talk to me or listen to what I had to say at the least. Deep inside I felt hopeless about my recurring dream of us getting married. I knew there wouldn't be a wedding day.

"I'm here to pick up a to-go order," a female voice beside me said.

I looked up to see Misty standing beside me. "Misty?"

"Jewel! Hey, girl!" She gave me a big hug.

"I've been trying to reach you. Haven't you gotten my calls and texts?"

"Yes, baby. I'm so sorry. I've been so busy. You wouldn't know all the things that have been going on."

"Jewel," another voice called out, interrupting me and Misty's conversation.

"Poppo," I answered, recognizing the voice.

"Hey, what's going on with the beautiful Jewel?" he asked.

"You got that right. I am beautiful," I responded, even though deep down I didn't truly feel that way.

Misty butted in quickly. "Well, I gotta run, girl."

"Oh, okay. I really wanted to sit and talk though."

"I'll call you as soon as I get a free moment. I promise." Misty grabbed her bag and rushed out of the restaurant.

"That's your girl?" Poppo asked after Misty walked away.

"Yeah. Why? You want to holla at her or something?"

"Oh, nah. I already tried. That bitch got a mouth on her that a make a nigga beat her ass."

"Why you say that? What did she say to you?"

"Well, that day I got locked up, I saw her at the jail, so I tried to holla. That bitch started talking some shit about me being a thug, and jail being my second home, straight dissing a nigga. Instead of cussing that bitch out, I just told her to have a nice day and walked off on her ass."

"Damn! Sorry about that. Maybe she was having a bad day. I wonder why she was at the precinct anyway. Hope nothing was wrong. She said a lot has happened to her in the past days. Now I'm worried. Give me a second. Let me call her."

I dialed Misty up.

This time she answered right away. "Hey, girl."

"Hey, Misty. Is everything okay? My friend just told me he saw you at the precinct not too long ago."

"Oh, girl, it was nothing. I had got locked up for a trespassing charge. I had seen my ex-boyfriend's car in front of this girl's house, so I went up there banging on the door, trying to get him to come out, and the bitch called the police on me. You know how that goes."

"Yeah, I do. Okay, hon. I'm not gonna hold you. Call me when you're free. We really need to catch up." I ended the call.

"Why you sitting at the bar by yourself?" Poppo asked as soon as I hung up the phone.

"I'm waiting for an order."

"Let me take care of that for you."

"Thanks." I grinned after the bartender brought my drink.

"Listen, ma, I'm glad that I ran into you. I got some good news for you."

"Well, it's about time. Go ahead, I'm listening." I nodded.

"I thought that nigga Calico was done when he got locked up, but he's going up for a bond hearing in a few days, and his lawyer is confident he's getting a bond. After he gets bonded out, I'm going to personally pick him up and handle things for you."

"Well, as long as you make shit happen, our deal is still good. Once Calico is out the way, I will put you on to one of my TMF connects." I assured Poppo as if my word was golden.

"Bartender, please . . . another drink for the lady. Now, you know I can't let you eat alone. You want to get a table?" Poppo asked.

"Sure." I giggled. It felt nice to have someone paying a little attention to me, especially since Touch wasn't even bothering to look my way.

At the table I noticed Poppo constantly staring into my eyes. "Why are you staring at me?" I blushed.

"It's not every day a man sees something as beautiful as you."

"Wow! You got a little game with you, huh?"

"This isn't game, baby. You can't appreciate those type of compliments because these lames you been fucking with don't know how to cherish a woman like you." Poppo grabbed my hand.

I didn't know how to respond to Poppo's comment.

In a way I took it as a diss because he was insinuating I have poor taste in men, but at the same time he was giving me a compliment by saying I was an exceptional woman. Since I didn't know what to say, I didn't say anything at all. I just smiled.

"If you were my woman, I would give you the world. You would never feel pain, hurt, sadness, or disappointment. You would always be on a pedestal."

Okay now, I knew this nigga was putting it on thick. He was talking straight bullshit. "Whatever." I knew exactly how to respond to that bullshit-ass statement.

"I know you feel like I'm just popping shit, but it's cool. I can show you better than I can tell you. That bitch nigga you with fucked your head up."

"Damn! You keep saying shit like I'm some sad case, a woman scorned or some shit. And why Touch gotta be a bitch?" I snapped. I was getting tired of Poppo's little comments, and he had crossed the line talking about Touch. I mean, I wasn't really feeling Touch, but I still loved him, and I wasn't gonna let no nigga diss him, especially no one from Calico's camp.

"Hold on, baby girl. Don't take offense. I'm just saying . . . I don't know what the next dude thought of you, but you're my dream woman, and by all means I would treat you like it. I would never take you for granted."

I thought, *Damn! Who the fuck is this nigga?* He was blowing me away. Just that quick, he'd made my whole attitude change. I didn't know if I'd just never given this nigga the opportunity to see what he was really like or if he was a different Poppo. Back in the day, I would have never even considered him an option, but this nigga really had me going. I didn't know if it was because I was so vulnerable from me and Touch's breakup, or if it was the alcohol, or if Poppo's game was just simply on point. I was actually starting to feel him a little bit. I needed to calm down.

"Miss, can I get another drink?" I was feeling a little tipsy, but I didn't care. After those days of pure hell I'd been through, I deserved to have a little fun. Poppo was saying all the right things, and I was sucking it all up.

"You want some more wings?" Poppo asked.

"Sure." I nodded. Not eating much in days, I guess I had worked up an appetite. When my emotions were out of whack, my body was too. My head, back, muscles, and joints all ached like I had the flu or something, when in reality it was all stress.

The waitress came back. "Here is your drink. Can I get you anything else?"

"Yes, she'll have another order of wings," Poppo said.

"With extra blue cheese dressing," I added before guzzling down yet another drink.

"Coming right up," the waitress said.

"You really want those wings," Poppo commented.

"Yes, I sure do. I probably could eat them all day." I giggled.

"Jewel, shit is about to be right for us," Poppo whispered in my ear, changing the subject.

"Okay." I laughed.

I was in no condition to discuss things further, but I

figured he was talking about money. Plus, I had to use the bathroom. All that alcohol I'd drank was going right through me.

"I appreciate your patience with the whole situation."

"No problem. I need to run to the bathroom."

I struggled to get up then stumbled, but Poppo caught me just in time before I fell to the ground.

"Maybe you should cool off with the alcohol. Why don't you go back to my house and chill? Are you all right to drive?"

"Yeah, I'm okay to drive to your house. I need a minute to use the bathroom," I said while he helped me there.

I had to admit, it was sweet that he was so concerned about me. The average nigga would have tried to keep me drinking, so they could get a "drunk fuck" out of me.

Chapter 25

"Making a Move"

Poppo

"Welcome to my home," I said to Jewel as we pulled up to a little spot I'd gotten in Norfolk.

I'd been spending so much time on the East Coast, and in VA in particular, I figured I may as well get a little spot. Hell, with the money I was spending in hotel costs every month, I may as well pay rent instead.

"Oh, this is cute! Looks just like a bachelor's pad." She giggled as we walked into the living room.

My living room was simple. I had a big-framed, black-and-white photo of Tony Montana from *Scarface* on the wall, a black leather sectional, and a 52-inch plasma on the wall. That's all a nigga needed.

"Make yourself comfortable." I handed Jewel the remote then headed to the kitchen to make her a drink. "What you want to drink?" I asked, trying to be a gentleman. If it was up to me alone, I would have given her a shot of Henny straight. That would have made my night go a lot easier.

"Uummm, what do you have?"

"Hennessy."

"That's it?"

"Look, ma, like you said, this is a bachelor's pad. I don't have no little sweet shit or none of that girly shit you be drinking."

"No Hpnotiq, Alizé, or Nuvo? Nothing?"

"Hpnotiq. But if you drink it, you have to drink an 'Incredible Hulk.' " I had to get the Henny in there some kind of way. You know that Henny make you sin, and that's exactly where I was trying to get to that night.

"Okay. Okay. Incredible Hulk it is." Jewel laughed and sat down on the couch, finally submitting.

"Here you go." I handed Jewel the drink then sat on the couch next to her.

"Thank you."

"Like I was saying in the restaurant, shit is about to come up for the both of us."

"Oh yeah? What makes you so sure?"

"Look, baby girl, I got my eyes on the prize, and by all means, I plan on getting it."

"So let me hear a little bit of this plan," Jewel said. "You got me real curious."

"All you need to know is, soon Calico is going to be six feet deep."

"Oh yeah? And what will happen after that?"

I knew exactly what Jewel wanted to hear, so I played

along. "I'm going to take the lead and be in charge. I'm already on my way. Since Calico's been locked up, I've been stacking dough and building up my new team. Some of the old team members will have to go because their loyalty will lie with Calico, and I can't have that. My empire will stand strong and make twice as much as his did. All I need is a queen bee like you by my side," I said, already beginning to feel on top of the world.

"Sounds like a good plan." Jewel guzzled down the drink I'd given her.

Ring! Ring!

My phone rang, interrupting our conversation. Normally I would have ignored it, but it was Murdock. That nigga owed me eighty-five hundred dollars, and I needed that shit, so I answered.

"Excuse me, ma. I need to answer this call," I said to Jewel then walked away. I picked up the call. "Yo?"

"Ready for you," Murdock said.

"I hope it's all there, Murdock. I ain't taking no cuts."

"I got eighty-five hundred for you."

"Cool. Meet me at KFC at Five Points," I instructed Murdock to meet me at a place close to the crib.

"Sorry about that, ma," I said to Jewel as I walked back into the living room. "Want to take a ride with me down the street real quick?" I asked her, knowing this would be the prefect opportunity to show her how I was getting money.

We hopped in the car, and I met up with Murdock at the KFC. He was already there when we pulled up. This time I got out of my car and hopped in with him.

Murdock handed me the money as soon as I got in. "Here you go."

"Eight-five hundred, right?" I tried to confirm, like always.

"It's all there, man," Murdock said. "And to show I'm a man about principle, I added a little interest."

"Thanks, but I don't need interest, nigga. I need you to pay on time." I then got out of his car and got back into mine.

"Count this for me." I handed Jewel the stack of money then pulled off. I watched as her eyes lit up and a broad smile came across her face.

"I don't count money unless it's mine." She smirked.

"Soon enough, baby girl, soon enough," I said, confident that the time when I could throw her stacks was near.

Minutes later we were back at my crib and comfortable on the couch like before.

"Would you like another drink?" I inquired as soon as we got settled. I already had a mixture of the Hennessy and Hpnotiq in a pitcher cooling in the fridge and ready to pour.

"Maybe just one more," Jewel said and turned on the television.

We were just in time to watch reruns of *The Game* on BET.

Ring! Ring!

My cell phone rang as I was making Jewel's drink. Not recognizing the number, I answered the phone in a fake voice. "Hello?"

158

"You gon' die, bitch nigga!" a male voice said from the other end.

"Oh yeah? You know where to find me," I said in a calm voice. "I ain't hiding." I then hung up the phone. I didn't want to draw any attention to my phone call and take the risk of ruining the mood me and Jewel had set so perfectly.

I'd been receiving those calls off and on since Deebo's death, and ain't shit happen. I had been carrying on with life as usual, and ain't shit jump off. Hell, those niggas knew where to find me if they really wanted some. The way I saw it, niggas was just popping shit, hoping to scare a nigga away.

I returned to the living room and handed Jewel her drink. "Here you go, sweetheart."

After Jewel finished that last drink, I didn't even bother to ask her if she wanted another one. I didn't want to make it seem like I was really trying to get her drunk. Maybe, she was done for the day and night.

I, on the other hand, knew how to hold my liquor and had about five Incredible Hulks with us just sitting on the couch. I was feeling nice and knew Jewel was feeling even better, so I didn't hesitate to make a move on her. I started by gently kissing her neck and feeling on her breasts. I wanted to put one in my mouth, but no sooner than I caressed her soft, supple breast, she shooed my hand away. Not wanting to ruin the mood and totally fuck things up, I eased off.

"How about a massage?" I whispered in her ear and

started to rub her shoulders before she could even respond.

She didn't resist, so I took that as my queue to keep going. I took my time, paying special attention to each part of her body as I rubbed her from head to toe. Although I was disappointed and nearly had blue balls, I was glad to have gotten this far. I just hoped the next time things would be different and I would be inside her pussy. I knew it was wet and juicy, and I couldn't wait for a taste. Literally!

Chapter 26

"Sweet Taste of Revenge"

Calico

Weeks had passed, and still no one had heard from Poppo's little bitch ass. I'd heard he'd gotten into a little beef on the streets and ended up killing the neighborhood bully, Deebo. That shit was a surprise to me. I guess he was really out there feeling himself, trying to act like he was the big man in town. The stories I was hearing about him really had me going. I couldn't believe this nigga really thought he was the boss. I was convinced he had bucked on me for my money and that was how he had his little come-up. I'd spent each day thinking about how the fuck I was gonna deal with him and was just hoping Deebo's boys didn't get to him first.

Bucking on my money was bucking on the Mexicans' money. And I didn't have the army to go to war with those niggas. Hell, I was already skating on thin ice, be-

161

cause Touch had fucked me up. I was just getting back in good with these niggas and wasn't trying to fuck it up all over again.

My first instinct was to just get out of jail, hunt his bitch ass down, and straight kill him, but then I started to think on a whole different level. After pulling a few strings, I was able to get one of his bitches in VA to give him a call on three-way. I finally had the opportunity to holla at that nigga.

Of course, I had to ask him about that shit with my baby mother first. That was a true violation. There is no way a nigga could feel up one of my chicks and get away with it, especially my baby moms. Then I asked about my money, and about the shit niggas was saying on the streets. And, like the bitch I knew he was, Poppo denied it all. He gave me some lame excuse about getting robbed, when it came to the money. He had managed to collect on half before he got robbed though. I made that nigga think everything was all good and there was no beef. Plus, when that nigga found out I had another bond hearing coming up and I was definitely getting out on that one, he straightened his act up. At first he thought I would never see daylight, so he was trying to flex. But when the reality hit that I was coming home, that nigga switched his whole shit up.

Just like Natalia had promised, I went before the judge and got a bond. I gathered my shit up, preparing to be released. A nigga never felt so happy. Two months in jail was way too much time for a cat like me. It took three different bond hearings for me to get a bond.

The judge set it at one million dollars, with hopes that I would never get out, but it only took one phone call and one hundred grand, and a nigga was on the road the same fucking day.

Now that I was hitting the streets, it was straight to business. I knew Poppo had to be dealt with. Then I had to get to that bitch Sasha before she got to the witness stand. She was the only eyewitness that had stepped up so far, so without her the Commonwealth's Attorney had no case.

When they released me, I walked out the gate and saw my baby mother parked outside.

"Hey, baby!" she ran up to me and gave me a big hug and kiss.

"What's up? I see you really love daddy, huh? You came all the way across the country to get your man. That's why I fuck with you so hard, Corrin." I gripped her ass and pulled her close to me, my dick swelling.

"Damn! Looks like you're not the only one that's happy to see me," she said, feeling my dick stand up against her thigh.

"So what you gonna do about that?"

"You'll see real soon. Get in the car. Let's get to our hotel."

I didn't hesitate to get in the car. Although I was horny as hell and wanted to fuck my baby mother more than anything, I can't lie, my mind was on other shit. Everything in me wanted to meet up with Poppo so I could give that nigga what he had coming to him.

Corrin drove us downtown Norfolk to the Waterside

Marriot, where she'd gotten the room. We pulled up in
front and let the valet park the car.

The door on the elevator hadn't even closed completely before she was all over me. She grabbed me by
my hair, which was now loose because I had taken out
my corn rolls while in jail. With a tight grip on my hair,
she forced her tongue in my mouth, pushing me against
the elevator wall.

I wrapped my arms around her and began to kiss her
back just as passionately. My dick was so hard, it felt like
it was going to explode. I turned around, pushing Corrin against the wall, then pushed my hands inside her
panties. Her pussy was hairless, and I instantly felt her
swollen clit between her fat pussy lips.

"Ahhhh, baby," she moaned. "Not in here." She
pulled my hand from her pants.

Ding!

The elevator sounded, letting us know we'd reached
our floor. Not knowing if someone would be standing
in front of us as the elevator door opened, we both
gathered ourselves. When the door opened, I followed
Corrin to the hotel room.

As soon as we got in, Corrin started to take her
clothes off. I followed her into the bedroom. By the
time we reached there, she was completely naked. I
grabbed her naked body and tossed it on the bed.

"No, baby, it's not time yet. First, you've got to get a
shower."

Corrin was tripping.

"Hell nah. You 'bout to give me this pussy. I've been

waiting months for some pussy, and you gon' tell me to go take a shower first?"

"Well, I'm getting in the shower. If you want me, you'll have to join me." She hopped up and ran into the bathroom.

I followed her in there. When I walked in, she was already in the shower. I ripped the curtain back and looked at her soaking wet, perfect body. Although she'd had two kids for me, her body was still flawless, not a stretch mark in sight. I pulled off my clothes and got in with her.

As soon as I stepped in, she grabbed a washcloth and soaped it up. Then she began to wash my body. From head to toe, Corrin wiped me down, not missing one spot. Then I stepped under the flow of the water to rinse the soap off.

When I turned around and all the soap was gone, Corrin got on her knees and began to suck my dick. I knew I was backed up, so when I felt the need to cum, I let the first one go and busted all in her mouth. Now that I'd gotten the quick one out of the way, it was time to really give it to her. My dick was still hard after I came.

I turned Corrin around and bent her over under the flow of water beneath the showerhead. I grabbed her by the waist and pushed my dick deep inside her.

"Aaahhh, fuck!" she screamed out.

Her pussy was nice and tight like always. Water splashed off her ass as I banged it. The sound and sight of her ass bouncing up and down turned me on even more. Before I knew it, Corrin had reached her peak, and I followed shortly after. Although exhausted, we both washed off one more time before getting out of the shower.

When we stepped out of the shower, room service was waiting on us. Corrin had ordered steak and lobster tail.

"I knew you would want something nice after eating jail food for so long," she said as she handed me my plate, "so I ordered the best."

"Damn, boo! You almost make me want to wife you up," I said, knowing that was what Corrin always wanted.

"That's what I'm waiting on. What is it gonna take, Mike?"

"Come on, Corrin, don't start. We're having a nice time, baby," I said, not wanting to hear the bullshit.

"Baby, me and the kids need you. This is the second time you've gone to jail. What if you don't get out the next time? What are we supposed to do without you?"

"Man, I ain't going nowhere. I got shit under control. You worrying for nothing." I didn't know why Corrin was so upset.

"See . . . that's what I mean. You think you're invincible. Mike, you're human. You bleed just like everyone else. It's time to leave the streets. You have money. I can work. I'm afraid, if you don't get out now, you're gonna end up dead or permanently in jail."

"Corrin, chill out." I kissed her on the cheek then picked up my phone to call Poppo.

"What up, nigga?" Poppo sounded excited to hear from me.

"I'm on the streets, nigga. Come get me from the Waterside Marriot. Call me when you're outside." I hung up the phone.

"Who was that?" Corrin was in my face again.

"Poppo," I said, my mouth full of food.

"Poppo? How the fuck could you even deal with that nigga, Mike? Especially after what he did to me?" She began to cry.

I hated to see her cry. "Baby, that nigga gonna pay for what he did, trust me. I would never let a nigga disrespect you and get away with it." I hugged her tight.

"Baby, please just don't get into any trouble."

"Don't worry, mama. I'll be back in Cali with you and the kids before you know it."

"You promise?"

"Only death could stop me." I then finished up my food.

Chapter 27

"Unexpected Guest"

Poppo

I'd just gotten a call from Calico to come pick him up. Truth be known, I was kind of disappointed that he had gotten out. I was enjoying being the king and running the castle. But so be it. This just meant I would have to hold true to my word and dead that nigga.

I stopped by the gas station to fill up the car and to grab a six-pack of Heineken for the road. I had a few in the car, but I needed to re-up for the trip. As I walked in, there was a sexy little petite chick that stood at the register. I gave her a smile as I headed toward the freezer to get the Heineken. She smiled back. That's all the confirmation I needed. I already knew I was gonna holla at her when I checked out.

I heard the lyrics of Soulja Boy's song, "Turn My Swag On," blasting from a car stereo outside the store. Shortly after, I heard a commotion at the front of the store. It sounded like a group of rowdy niggas had just walked in.

"What up, sexy?" one of the guys said, obviously speaking to the cashier at the front of the store.

Another one of the boys sang out the lyrics of Soulja Boy's song. He sounded like he was getting closer to me.

Eager to get the fuck out of the store, I grabbed up the Heineken and headed to the front of the store. No sooner than I got to the end of the aisle, I caught eyes with one of the guys. He stood at the other end of the aisle. I recognized him immediately as one of Deebo's boys.

We locked eyes, like a cowboy stand-off, and before I could blink, he fired a shot at me. One hit the case of Heineken, busting the bottles and causing them to drop out of my hand.

I dove to the next aisle and grabbed my gun. I met the guy at the front of the store, and we fired shots at each other, as his boy ran out the front door. Moments later, he followed behind him and jumped in the truck. I ran out the door after them.

On the way out, I noticed the cashier laid out on the floor, blood coming from her chest. She had been shot.

I jumped in my car and followed the SUV Deebo's boys were driving. I got up close enough to them to fire some shots. One shot hit a tire, almost sending the SUV out of control for a second.

I pressed the pedal to the floor, determined to catch up with them. As soon as I got by their side, the driver quickly busted a right turn and ended up losing control of the truck, which flipped over into the ditch.

I pulled over beside them. I saw the driver crawling from the truck and gave him two shots. I was sure that nigga wouldn't be breathing after that.

With no time to waste, I jumped back in my car and sped off, leaving no eyewitnesses behind. I had to make sure I put those niggas to rest, to let niggas on the street know what was really good. It took shit like that to get a name.

Now that I had a couple of murders under my belt, I was sure I would be respected on the streets. Money, power, and respect was all it took to be the boss. I had the money, and with money came power, and now I had finally gained the respect.

Chapter 28

"Handling Business"

Calico

"Gotdamn! What up, big homie?" I dapped up Poppo. "Take me straight to the *A*," I said to him as we hopped in the car.

Once I was in the *A*, Poppo would be easily dealt with. Then I would hunt down Sasha. If I didn't take care of Sasha, I knew I may never have a chance to shower, eat, or fuck on my own will again.

"Damn, nigga! You on a mission. You trying to holla at Diablo, or you trying to get at that bitch, Sasha?"

"My main thang is Sasha, but I'm gonna holla at Diablo too. I gotta do something to make up for that dough you fucked up. How that shit happen though . . . on the real, man?"

"Man, I hooked up with some of these other ATL cats. The first go-'round I gave these niggas half of the shit, and everything went straight. Then next time I met up with them to get rid of the rest, these niggas was on some other shit. They straight robbed me, man."

"What the fuck you doing dealing with them anyway? The plan was for you to deal with Diablo, man."

"I know, but I could sell it to these niggas for a little more."

"Oh, so you was trying to make a little profit of your own. See where greed get you? Nigga, you ain't ready to be no fucking boss, so stop trying to act like one!" I snapped.

"A'ight, duke." Poppo ended the argument.

The more I looked at Poppo, the angrier I got. I'd managed to deal with it nearly the entire drive, but that last thirty minutes was killing me. I was ready to take him out. I was just waiting for the perfect opportunity.

"Yo, can you get a Heineken for me out of the backseat?" Poppo whined.

"Yeah," I replied, realizing this may be the opportunity I'd been waiting for.

In jail, a nigga can get anything he wants. I was lucky enough to run into this dude that mixed up a number of prescription meds to make this drug that paralyzes a person for at least six hours or so. It was the jail version of the street drug "Special K." Special K was actually a drug used to tranquilize cats.

I popped open a Heineken for Poppo and put in a little bit of the drug and handed it to him. Pretending like I was actually concerned about Poppo drinking and driving, I suggested I take over the driving from that point.

"Man, I've been locking shit down while you were gone," he bragged.

"Oh yeah? How the fuck you lock shit down?" I knew this nigga was a little bitch and didn't have the balls to put a city on lock.

"Nigga, I knocked off Deebo. Niggas thanking me to this day. That nigga was going around taking niggas' money and drugs and shit. Ain't nobody have the balls to stand up to that nigga. But I ain't back down. Instead, I made that nigga lay down."

"Yeah. I heard about that shit when I was locked up. I wondered what the fuck was going on."

"Nigga tried to bitch me out during a dice game, so I had to let that nigga know. You know what I mean?"

Poppo was going on like he really was the man on the streets.

"Right, right," I said, making him feel a little good.

"Then I got word that his boys were after me. Niggas was calling my phone, threatening me and shit, but I was like, 'Fuck it! Y'all niggas know where to find me. I ain't hiding. So days had passed, and I ain't never see none of these niggas, that is until tonight."

"Tonight? You ran into these niggas before you came to pick me up?" Now I was really interested in what Poppo had to say.

"Yeah, man. I was at the fucking gas station, and these niggas rolled up on me. They started busting shots and shit, even hit the cute little cashier bitch. Anyway, I catch up with these niggas about a mile from the gas station. They had flipped the truck and shit, so when the nigga come crawling out the truck, I hit him with a couple of shots."

"So that nigga dead?"

Totally ignoring my question, Poppo called out in a panic, "Yo, I can't move my legs."

That was my queue. It didn't even take ten minutes before that shit I put in his drink started to work.

"Pretty soon you won't be able to move your arms either." I gave him a devious grin.

"What did you do to me?"

"Shut the fuck up!" I yelled and punched him in the mouth. Afterwards, my hand hurt like hell.

Shortly after, we arrived at an abandoned warehouse. I came across it on our last visit to Atlanta. The only things there were spiders and rats. I pulled Poppo's still paralyzed body from the car and dumped it on the dirty warehouse floor. Then I placed duct tape around his arms and legs. I'd had him purchase all the equipment prior to picking me up, so we would be prepared for Sasha. Little did this punk know it was for him.

In the warehouse, I started cutting him on his arms, legs, face, fingers, and neck. Finally, I took off his shirt and cut his chest and stomach open. For a while, I let him bleed out. That nigga looked petrified. I took my time torturing him before I began to speak.

"What? You thought you would get away at trying to duck me and play with my fucking money? Not to mention, you violated me by putting your hands on my baby moms. That alone is a death sentence, bitch nigga! Did you forget where you came from nigga? You were no-body. I made you, Poppo. When we met, you were on the corner selling nicks and dimes, nigga. I opened the doors for you." I kicked him in the head. I couldn't be-lieve this ungrateful-ass nigga.

"Fuck you, Calico! I ain't your bitch. I just ain't have the chance to prove it to your ass. You suppose to be dead right now, nigga. I had plans for you. You never was suppose to leave Bankhead. If that stupid-ass crack-head hadn't fucked up, you wouldn't be here right now!"

"So what the fuck you saying, Poppo? You tried to fucking set me up?" Furious, I kicked him two more times.

Poppo began to laugh. Then he coughed up blood. "Why you think your gun jammed?" he forced out the words then spat out blood. "I had given the crackhead a gun to pull on you and force you in the house, then from there, I was gonna take over. I made sure the gun would jam because I knew you would pull it out on him. But like a typical fucking crackhead, this nigga sold the gun and decided to try and rob you at knifepoint in-stead."

"Fuck you, nigga!"

I'd heard enough, so with gloves on and his own gun, I shot him twice in the head and left him as a nice snack for the rats.

Now that I had one task down, it was time to move on to the other. I needed to holla at Diablo. According to

Poppo, Sasha was working for Diablo, so I knew as long as I was fucking with him, I was guaranteed to run into that bitch.

"What up, Diablo?" I shouted out the window to him as I pulled up in front of the club.

He spoke to me through the window. "What's up, man?"

"Hop in, so I can holla at you."

Diablo walked over to the passenger side and hopped in. I wanted to waste no time getting right down to business. I knew I would have to come at this nigga right, so I would be able to get the information I needed. But before I could begin to speak, Diablo started talking.

"Yo, nigga, I need you bad right now. I just took a major loss."

"For real? Damn, man! That's how the game go. What you looking for?"

"Well, I was hoping I could give you something, and you match what I buy. You dig?"

"A'ight, I can work with that. But I need to ask you about this chick you work with . . . Sasha."

"Sasha? Man, you don't want to deal with that conniving bitch."

Diablo had just made my job a whole lot easier. I was thinking I was gonna have to act like I wanna use the bitch as a runner or some bullshit, to get info from that nigga, but it looked like Sasha had rubbed this nigga the wrong way.

"What's up with her man?" I asked, wanting Diablo to elaborate.

"She's the reason I'm fucked up right now. I gives this bitch some weight to take to my niggas in VA, and she calls me, saying, this nigga Touch robbed her. So I goes up there ready for war and roughs this nigga up. I shot after him and everything. On top of that, I still had to straighten these niggas that didn't get their shit, because they had already given me the money. So a few days later, I get a call from these same niggas, saying, they just bought some cheap shit from some niggas that robbed a bitch. When they described the bitch, I knew it was none other than Sasha. The puzzle just fit together way too perfectly. The bitch had lied. Touch ain't rob her. That bitch robbed me!"

"Oh yeah? So now you and this nigga Touch got beef?"

"Hell yeah. Now that's some extra shit I gotta deal with, on top of the loss I took."

"I know that nigga Touch. Me and him had a little run-in too," I said, not sharing too much information. "So about this bitch, Sasha . . . have you talked to her?"

"Nah. I don't want her to know I know what's up. I'm trying to get her here so I can deal with her. I've been calling her, telling her I got more work for her, but she dragging her feet getting here. She suppose to blow in tomorrow though."

"How about this? Get her here, and I'll deal with her for you." I offered to take the problem off of Diablo's hands without telling him my personal beef with her.

"Done deal. I'll let you know when she's at the club, and you get at me about that other thang when you ready. Or you gonna send your boy Poppo? Where that nigga at anyway? I been trying to holla at him since that shit went down."

"Poppo? That nigga ain't breathing," I said with no emotion at all.

"Huh? Fuck you talking about Calico?" Diablo laugh nervously.

"I gutted him." Again I had a completely blank face.

Diablo didn't respond. He wasn't sure how to take me. He just stared at me speechless, looking totally confused.

"I'm fucking with you, nigga. He straight," I said, breaking the ice.

"Man, you had me fucked up. I'm gone." Diablo dapped me up and got out of the car.

I pulled out of the parking lot, pleased that things were falling into place.

Chapter 29

"A Day Full of Surprises"

Jewel

It had been weeks since I'd seen or heard from Touch. The last time I saw him was the night he left the house, crushing any hopes I had of us reuniting. Although it wasn't an easy task, I'd managed to stop calling his phone twenty times a day and thinking about him every minute of the hour.

My days were long and lonely, but I was determined to get over him. I did as many things as I could to stay occupied. The house was spotless, because I'd used cleaning as one of my distractions. I'd gone as far as to even clean out our closets, pantry, and cupboards. When I wasn't cleaning, I was working out or at the gym taking a swim.

Weeks earlier, all of my time was wasted planning for my wedding, but since it was pretty obvious no wedding was in my future, I'd stopped all proceedings. I'd even tried to collect refunds on some of my deposits.

Although Touch wasn't around, and there was no money coming in, the bills didn't stop accumulating. Touch and I had accrued quite some debt with our ghetto-fabulous lifestyle, and our bank account was getting smaller and smaller each day. I didn't know what the future had in store. It even crossed my mind to contact my boy from TMF to do a little business transaction of my own.

I checked the mail to see what new bills had come through. As I sat at the breakfast bar and flipped through the bills, my stomach turned. I literally became nauseous. I jumped from the barstool and rushed to the downstairs bathroom.

"*Blaugh!*" I began to vomit in the toilet.

I'd been experiencing nausea and fatigue for the past couple of days. At first, I thought I was coming down with a stomach virus, but it was too sporadic. I'd even tried calling Misty to get her medical advice, but I had not even talked to her that much since the night Touch left. I'd left numerous messages, but she hadn't returned any of them. She hadn't even returned my text messages. I wondered if I'd done something wrong or if she was mad at me. It was like she and Touch both walked out my life at the same time.

Not knowing what else to do, I decided to try the obvious and take a pregnancy test. I unwrapped the wrapper and placed the tip of the test under a stream of my urine, as the instructions stated. I recapped the tip and washed my hands and waited.

Two minutes seemed like two hours, but when it was over, I rushed over to read the results. I glanced down and read the results. Unsure if what I was seeing was correct, I picked the test up and read it a little closer.

"Oh, God!" I screamed then burst into tears.

I dropped the test on the floor then slid down in a corner of the bathroom. I sat there with my knees bent to my chest and buried my head in my arms and sobbed uncontrollably. I couldn't understand what I had done so bad that God was punishing me like this. In a matter of weeks, I'd lost my future husband, become distant with my new best friend, and now I was going to be forced to raise a child alone. There was no way I was prepared to raise a child. I had neither security nor the slightest idea how to even raise a damn child.

I gathered myself and tried to call Misty again. I really hated to bother her, because I'd called so many times already, but I really needed someone to talk to. I felt like I was literally on the verge of a nervous breakdown.

"Hey, girl," Misty answered right away.

I was relieved to hear her voice. "Hey, Misty. I really need to talk. I've been trying to reach you for some time now."

"I know, I know. I'm so sorry, boo. I've been working overtime at the hospital, so I've been so exhausted. In fact, I'm on my way in right now. I'll call you when I get off."

"Okay," I said, although I was quite disappointed that I hadn't a chance to tell her what was going on with me.

Stressed, exhausted, and just plain old depressed, I drank a cup of Sleepytime tea and laid down for a nap.

Bang! Bang! Bang!

I was wakened by a hard, constant banging on the front door.

Three Virginia Beach police officers were at the door.

"Yes," I answered.

"Are you California Jewel Diaz?" one of the police officers asked.

"Who? No, you have the wrong house." I backed up and slammed and locked the door in their faces.

It was a dead bolt, so they were going to have to break the door down. I ran upstairs to grab my purse and raided the sock drawer to see what cash I had in there. I didn't have much time.

While the cops were desperately trying to get my front door open, I quickly ran downstairs and headed out of the back kitchen door.

A police officer greeted me with a 9 millimeter gun in my face. "Get down on the ground!" he ordered.

Another one cuffed me. "You're under arrest for conspiracy to distribute narcotics. Where is Trayvon Davis?"

The third police officer started reading me my Miranda rights, as the other officers rushed through the house looking for Touch.

I was speechless. I couldn't believe what was going on. I sat silent as a mouse as those pigs threw me in the police car to take me down to the station.

Chapter 30

"On a Mission"

Touch

Days had passed since I'd fucked Misty, but something about her just didn't sit well with me. I couldn't understand how this bitch was supposed to be Jewel's girl, yet she gave the pussy up so easily. I couldn't help but think about Sasha when I thought about Misty. Those two bitches were one and the same.

I actually started to feel sorry for Jewel. She had the worst luck, when it came to females.

As I pulled into the driveway, I decided to give her a call. Her cell phone went straight to voicemail, so I tried calling the house. When I called the house, the phone rang out until voicemail picked up. It had been a couple days since I'd last received a call from Jewel. I'd originally figured she had finally gotten some pride and decided to stop calling, but when I called her and wasn't able to reach her, something came over me.

Deep inside, I felt something was wrong. I got out of my car and headed to my front door.

"Yo, Touch," my neighbor called out to me.

I stopped in the driveway to speak to him. "What's up, man?"

"The police was at your crib today, man. They was out here asking niggas when the last time you been here and shit."

I didn't know what the fuck was up, but I wasn't taking no chances in finding out. I'd already planned to take a trip to the *A* to deal with this nigga Diablo, but the information my neighbor shared with me had instantly put those plans into motion.

I didn't even bother going into my crib. After talking to my neighbor, I walked right back to my car and got right back in.

I called up Lisa.

"Hey, boo." She sounded excited to hear from me.

"What's up, baby?"

"Nothing. Chilling. What's up with you?"

"I need a favor, ma."

"Okay. What's up? You know you can always depend on me, even though you be putting me through hell with all your bitches."

"Ah shit! There you go. How many times I gotta apologize?"

"Mmmm . . . maybe about ten to fifteen more times." Lisa giggled.

"Look, on the real, though, I need you to switch cars with me for a few days."

"Oh, no problem. I don't mind pushing the seven forty-five. But the question is, what is your bitches gonna say? I don't want no beef, Touch."

"Everything good, man. I'm on my way over." I hung up the phone.

When I got to Lisa's house, it took about ten minutes for me to bend her over and get a quickie. Then I switched cars with her, and I hopped on the interstate and headed to Atlanta.

My brain was racing the entire ride there. I tried calling Jewel several times, but I still couldn't get her. Then I began to think even harder. I started to wonder if this bitch had set me up. I knew bitches had a habit of letting their emotions take over and doing some crazy shit. That would explain why she stopped calling me and wasn't answering any of my calls.

My mind ran on Misty. *What if that bitch set me up? She knew a little too much about me, and the bitch just came on the scene out of nowhere.* At that point everybody was a suspect. I broke my phone in two and threw it out the window onto Interstate 95.

The longer I drove, the more I was consumed with my thoughts. I tried to listen to the radio and CDs, but nothing could get my mind off this shit. *This is what I get for thinking with my dick. I should have never fucked that girl, Misty. I didn't even know that broad like that. What if Jewel found out we had sex and now she's out to get me? These bitches had me slipping.*

I was disappointed with myself. I was usually on point with shit, but I had to admit, I'd fucked up a whole lot in those past few weeks. I knew when I got to the *A*, I would need to get one of those pre-paid cell phones to conduct my business, but first I needed to pay a visit to Diablo.

It worked out in my favor that I got to Atlanta late that night. I went to a strip club called Bottoms Up that I frequented. I figured I would catch Diablo there. The last time I ran into him, it was at that same spot.

Sure enough, just like I figured, he was there. I discreetly sat in the corner of the club and waited patiently for an hour for him to head out.

I watched him stagger to his car. I pulled out of the parking lot behind him. He was too drunk to realize I was even following him. Plus, I was thankful he didn't take no bitches home with him. The less witnesses, the better for me. Besides, the only one whose head I wanted to put a bullet in was Diablo's.

Diablo pulled up in his garage. Just as he was closing the garage door, I literally rolled my body in underneath it before it shut. When I pressed up on him, his back was turned.

"Nigga, what the fuck you doing here?" he asked before I put my gun into his back.

"You don't get to ask any questions." Without warning, I shot him in the leg.

"Man, you shot me!" he whimpered in surprise.

"Do we understand each other? Next time, I have no problem with shooting you in the throat."

"Yeah, I got you." He nodded, sweat coming from his forehead.

"Take me to your basement." I shoved him in the back with my gun.

I followed a limping Diablo through his house and into his basement. Once there, I tied him up with some rope he had on the counter in his basement and got ready for his execution.

"Touch, man, please don't kill me," he begged. "I got kids."

"There you go again with your mouth." I pistol-whipped him.

"Please," he said, blood pouring down the side of his face.

"Why you think I stole from you, bitch nigga? I run these fucking streets. You really think I need to steal from you?" I asked.

"Sasha told me you robbed her. That shit was worth eighty grand. But I later found out that bitch kept the shit and tried selling it to some niggas in VA. I guess she set us both up, man. The bitch is sheisty. Maybe she was thinking one of us would be in a six-feet-deep grave right now. Please—"

"Nigga, shut the fuck up! Crying like a little bitch!" I untied him enough where he could maneuver his way out of the ropes. Then I quickly dipped out of his crib.

I knew deep inside this nigga was telling the truth. One, I knew how this bitch Sasha moved, and two, just how that shit happened didn't seem right. First, the bitch was trying to get a piece of my dick. Then as soon as I diss her, this nigga was calling up saying I robbed Sasha. That bitch just saw an opportunity for get-back and to make some cash all at the same time.

Chapter 31

"Payback's a Bitch"

Calico

"Yo," I answered Diablo's call, hoping he was gonna deliver the message I'd been waiting for.

"She's ready for you."

"Cool. I'm on my way."

I'd waited nearly two weeks for Sasha to arrive in Atlanta. For a moment I had thought about going to VA to look for her ass. Luckily, I waited a few extra days.

I jumped in my car and headed to the club, where I slid in unnoticed, trying to draw as little attention to myself as possible.

The scene was the same as the very first time I'd gone there. There was a group of guys in one corner playing Madden on the projector screen, another set gambling in another corner, and Diablo was in another spot, having a conversation with another cat.

Just like before, I entered the dice game. After about fifteen minutes, I heard niggas talking about a phat ass that just bounced into the club, so I turned around to check out the ass too.

Bingo, I thought, a smile spreading across my face. That phat ass looked real familiar to me. I was almost certain it belonged to Sasha.

To be sure, I pulled out my cell phone and scrolled down to the name Malibu then hit *send.* Moments later, her phone began to ring, and she started to fumble through her purse to search for it. Already having my confirmation, I hung up.

I sat quiet as a mouse, watching Sasha's every move. She didn't look in the direction of the dice game, so she didn't even notice me.

When I saw her leave the club, I slipped out of the club and cautiously made my way to the car and jumped in. I noticed a staggering Diablo right behind me.

"What the fuck happen to you, man?" I asked as soon as he got in the car.

"I got shot."

"What? Man, get the fuck out of the car! I can't be taking no cripple with me on no shit like this," I said, not willing to take any risks.

"Chill out, man. Everything a'ight."

"Yeah, okay, nigga. Shit get tight, you on your own."

"I can hold my own, man. Don't worry about me."

That ended the conversation as we spotted Sasha loading the duffle bag Diablo had given her in the trunk of her car. I waited until she left the parking lot and followed her for more than twenty minutes, waiting for the right time to let her have it.

"Looks like she's headed to her crib," Diablo said. "We gonna have to be careful because she has two little boys, and sometimes her baby daddy be there."

I watched as she pulled onto a quiet neighborhood street then into an apartment complex. Sasha grabbed her duffle bag and headed into her third-floor apartment.

Minutes later, we grabbed our guns and rushed to her apartment.

I kicked the door in. I was the first to spot her. "Surprise, surprise, bitch!" I said, pointing the gun in her face.

"What the fuck is this?"

Smack!

I hit her hard in the face with the gun, and she dropped to the floor.

"Shut the fuck up, bitch!" Diablo pinned her to the living room wall. "I ought to kill your muthafuckin' ass."

I punched her in the face. "How long did you think you was going to keep playing us and we not figure out your damn scheme?" This bitch deserved to get beat like a dude. She thought she was so fucking slick, taking other people's money.

Diablo still had her pinned to the wall.

"Please . . . my sons are in the other room sleeping. Don't hurt them," she begged, almost breathless.

"Let her go," I ordered Diablo, and she fell helpless

to the ground, choking and trying desperately to catch her breath. "I got something better in store for this bitch." I snatched her shirt off, leaving her in her bra. "You want to see what it feels like to have something precious taken from you?" I slid my gun beneath her bra, forcing her breasts to pop out.

Sasha tried desperately to crawl away. "Please don't do this."

Wham! I kicked her one time in the stomach.

As she balled up in the fetal position, I lifted her skirt and began to unbutton my pants. I was gonna teach her a lesson.

I glanced over to see Diablo standing in the corner like a scared little bitch.

I forced her legs open. My dick was rock-hard as I slid her panties off, leaving her completely naked.

"Mommy," a little boy called out, rubbing his eyes.

Without flinching, I shot him in the head one time.

"No, not my baby! Nnnnooooo! He didn't deserve that!" Sasha screamed out, trying to fight with all her might.

Now that shit had turned in a different direction, sex was no longer a priority. I needed to get the money and get the fuck out. Besides, Diablo looked as though he was gonna pass out at any moment.

I kicked Sasha in the stomach again. "Where's the money?"

"My baby!"

"Where's the fuckin' money?" I followed with three more kicks to the stomach.

"Oh my God!"

"Where's my muthafuckin' money, bitch?" I punched her in the head to help her remember where it was.

"All right, all right, I will get it for you. It's in the living room closet," she informed us and began slowly crawling in that direction.

Diablo and I quickly went to the living room and opened the closet door. We began to search through all the shit stacked up in the closet.

"It's near the back," she said between tears.

After ransacking the closet for a few minutes and still not finding shit, I started to feel like this bitch was trying to play me. I turned around, planning to go and shoot this bitch's other son, to let her know this shit wasn't a game, but to my surprise when I turned around, she was gone.

I looked up just in time to see her climbing over the balcony. I started firing shots, and this crazy bitch straight jumped, never looking back or thinking twice.

Diablo and I rushed over and looked from the balcony of the apartment to see a lifeless body covered in blood. I would have shot that bitch again, but from the looks of things, there was no need. That bitch was definitely gone, her body twisted like a pretzel and blood flowing all around her.

Almost instantly, people started to crowd around her and yell out for help. The last thing my ass needed was even more witnesses to get rid of.

Diablo and I got the fuck out of there. This shit was spiraling out of control. We ran down the stairs, but when we reached the bottom, police were already pulling up. There was no way we could make it to the car, so our only option was to make a run for it. Knowing Diablo would only slow me up, I dipped off, leaving him alone. He didn't even resist, and the cops arrested him right away.

The cops were right on my heels.

"Get down! Put down your weapon!"

There was no way I could go down. This time for sure I would never see daylight. Not even Natalia would be able to get me out of this one. So, with no other option left, I decided to shoot my way out. It was do or die.

I stopped in my tracks, turned around, and faced the cops. They all froze and pointed their guns right at me. I said a silent prayer and slowly lifted my gun.

Bam! Bam! Bam! Bam! Bam! Bam!

It seemed like shots rang out forever, my body gyrating and burning all over. I knew I was taking my last breath and this was lights out.

Chapter 32

"Life on the Run"

Touch

Looking down at my watch, the clock read a little after midnight. Going down 95 South was easy and smooth for me, but coming back up 95 North was a muthafucker. At least five damn times, I almost fell asleep at the wheel. The last time I dozed off, I veered to the left and woke up in time to barely miss the deep ridges on the side of the road, which scared the hell out of me. One thing for sure, those things definitely worked. Otherwise, my ass would have come off the highway and ended up in the ditch.

I turned on some country music and rolled down every window in the car as I continued my drive. I knew once I got on Route 58 East, it would be smooth sailing from there.

My plan was to go chill at Lisa's house for a while and

lay low. I needed to get my mind right and sort some things out. I called her up to run things by her.

"Hey, boo," she greeted me on the phone.

"You home?"

"Well, I was just about to go out with my girls downtown and barhop. What's up?"

"I want to come through for a while."

"That's cool. I should be back home in a couple of hours."

"Tell you what . . . if you stay home and wait for me in that red piece you wore last time, I'll stop by and grab a to-go order for you at IHOP. Don't worry, I know you like your bacon extra crispy."

"You know that's one of my favorite spots. Let me call my girlfriends and tell them I won't be coming out tonight. Don't keep me waiting too long," she cooed.

"Give or take, I'll be about an hour," I assured her and hung up the phone.

Out of my left rearview mirror, I noticed this black Tahoe had been following me ever since I'd passed Emporia. At the time I was almost to Suffolk. It wasn't unusual for a person to be behind you for a while, because Route 58 was such a long stretch, but I didn't want to take any chances.

I pressed on the gas pedal and moved up to eighty miles per hour. The Tahoe did the same. I moved up to ninety and hauled ass. When I saw they were still keeping up, I was sure I was being followed.

Not knowing if these were some of Diablo's niggas or

someone from Calico's crew, I pulled out my gun and cocked it.

I slowed down a little, prepared to bust shots all up in that fucking truck, but to my surprise, as soon as I slowed down, sirens began to go off. I looked in the rearview to see blue and red flashing lights on the dashboard of the truck. It was the fucking police in an unmarked car!

My forehead was sweating, and my heart felt as though it was beating out of my chest, but I couldn't lose focus. I continued to keep my eye on the Tahoe and on the road.

I moved up to ninety-five miles per hour. I wasn't going to let those fucking pigs take me in without a fight, and throw me in a urine-infested cell. I drove like a crazed man, swerving around cars.

In no time I was in Portsmouth. I knew a few spots I could definitely dodge the fucking police in that area, especially since it was only one truck after me.

I didn't know if this nigga thought he was "Supercop" or what, but he never called for backup. Shit like that made me think they wanted to do a nigga in. With no backup, he could kill me and then say it was in self-defense. You never could tell when it came to cops these days.

I noticed an exit ramp a short distance ahead. I hopped on the ramp, doing ninety, not letting up on speed the least little bit.

Just as I was going around the curve on the ramp, I looked up to see a fucking Honda Accord coming the wrong way. It was coming right at me. With no time to stop, I swerved to avoid hitting it.

Unfortunately, the black Tahoe behind me wasn't so lucky. All I heard was a loud crash then I saw the Tahoe go up into the air and flip over at least four times. Then the Tahoe rolled and landed with the tires up.

Damn! That nigga gotta be good as dead. I breathed a sigh of relief.

My next stop was IHOP and then to Lisa's house.

Chapter 33

"Judgment Day"

Jewel

My stomach was in knots as I entered the courtroom and sat at the defendant's table with my lawyer. I didn't know if it was anxiety, or my baby doing flips in my stomach, but I surely felt sick. Minutes later, the prosecutor came and sat across from me at his table. Then came the judge.

I took a deep breath as the prosecution began.

"Your Honor, we would like to request a continuance. There's been a tragic accident. Our key witness has been killed in the line of duty. Melissa Johnson, the lead detective on this case, had gathered an enormous amount of evidence and tapes that led to the indictments for California Jewel Diaz, AKA Jewel, Trayvon Davis, AKA Touch, and several members of the True Mafia Family, AKA TMF. Without her here to testify, the prosecution needs a little more time to develop a stronger case."

My attorney stood up to speak. "Your Honor, the defense would like to request a bond until the next trial date."

"Continuance granted. Bond set at one hundred thousand dollars," the judge said then dismissed court.

Luckily I'd grabbed the money Touch and I had in the stash. Plus, I had gotten refunds on some of the deposits I'd paid for the wedding. That money, added to my little nest egg I had saved up for emergencies, was just enough for me to make bond. Hours later, I was on my way home.

I took a deep breath as I placed my key in the door and walked in my house. A part of me screamed, *Home, sweet home*, while another part of me wanted nothing to do with that house or any of the memories that came along with it. I made my way through the mess the cops left behind while searching the house, and found a comfortable spot on the couch in the living room.

I flipped on the television and heard the reporter say, *"Lead detective in big conspiracy case killed in the line of duty."*

Knowing this was my case they were referring to, I turned up the volume on the television. I watched as they showed the pictures from the scene of the crime. It was a bad accident on the exit ramp of the interstate. They showed pictures of a black Tahoe that was flat as a pancake. It looked like it had flipped over like six times. Evidently the officer was on a high-speed chase when a drunk driver came up the exit ramp and hit her head-on.

When they flashed a picture of the detective on the screen, my mouth dropped to the floor. I rubbed my eyes to make sure I wasn't hallucinating.

"Melissa Johnson was in pursuit of a wanted felon by the name of Trayvon Davis, AKA Touch when . . ."

The rest of the words the reporter spoke were a blur. My brain wandered elsewhere. *Misty, nurse Misty, wedding planner Misty, my so-called best friend Misty was an undercover police!* Everything in me just wanted to burst into tears. *How could I have been so stupid? I knew better. I'd already gone through this with Sasha, and Touch had warned me from day one. But I didn't listen.*

I began to feel like all of this was my fault. I broke the rules of the game. I let that bitch come into our lives, and day by day she tore it up, leaving me facing conspiracy charges, broke, and pregnant, with my baby father on the run.

My heart suddenly ached for Touch, so I called him up.

"Hello?" he answered on the first ring.

I burst into tears. Just the sound of his voice was so comforting. "Touch."

"What's up, Jewel? What's wrong, baby girl?"

"Touch, I miss you. I need you. *We* need you."

"Jewel, I can't even lie to you. I miss you too. I even tried calling you, but you didn't answer my calls."

"Touch, I was in jail. I've been through so much. You have put me through so much. You don't understand how this shit has torn me apart. I went days without eating, and nights without sleeping."

"I'm sorry, Jewel. I swear, I'm sorry. What happened? What the fuck were you doing in jail?"

"The police came here with an indictment on conspiracy charges. They had one for you too."

"Yeah, I heard. My neighbor told me they came to my crib. What the fuck is going on? This shit is crazy."

"Touch, you're all over the news."

"What the fuck?"

"Yes, you are. You were in a high-speed chase last night?"

"Yeah."

"Well, do you know who was following you?"

"No."

"It was Misty."

"Misty?" Touch said in a confused tone.

"Yes, Touch. She was an undercover police officer the entire time. She set us up. I feel so responsible. I should have never let her in. You warned me time and time again. This is all my fault." I began to cry even more.

"Nah, baby. It's not just you. I'm just as much to blame. Now I just gotta make shit right."

"Yes, you do. Please make things right." I then said again, "We need you here with us."

Touch finally caught on. "Why do you keep on saying that? Who is *we*?"

"*We* is me and your unborn child."

"My unborn child?"

"Yes, Touch. I'm pregnant."

Touch didn't say anything, and for a moment, we sat on the phone in silence.

I finally spoke up. "So what do we do now?"

"We be a family. I'm on my way home." Touch hung up the phone.

For the first time in days, I had a smile on my face.